FABULIST & FANTASTICAL WORLDS

A SHORT STORY COLLECTION

JOYCE REYNOLDS-WARD

FOREWORD

Welcome to my collection of fabulist and fantasy stories! As I put this collection together, I realized that many of the short stories I've published over the years frequently involve transformations or changes. Many of these stories would fit in our current world...except for that little twist that makes them not quite of this world, either.

Some of these stories are on the lighter side. Others are not.

Enjoy!

THE LIGHTER SIDE...

I

J.C. THE SKI BUM

"Jesus taught me how to ski," the kid in the bright orange ski pants said to the middle-aged lady next to me on the chairlift.

She barked a sharp but friendly laugh. "You mean Haysus, don't you? Didn't know they had a Latino ski instructor up here." She waved a hand toward the day lodge, the bright lights for night skiing casting shadows on the run below us.

"No bullshit," the kid insisted, pushing his goggles up onto his camouflage ski helmet. "Jesus. No Latino guy, the real thing. As in Jesus the Christ, the Son of God."

"Come on," the lady bantered. "You can't convince me of *that* chunk of blarney, Thomas."

"No, really, Mrs. K. Jesus's a ski instructor up here. How else did I learn to ski so well in two seasons?" Thomas scratched the scraggly soul patch on his chin.

"You're a natural athlete, kiddo," Mrs. K said, shaking her head. "Even if you *are* full of BS."

"For real, Mrs. K!"

"Tell me another one, Thomas. I might just believe *that*."

We approached the ramp. Mrs. K put up the bar, sliding off easily with Thomas and turning left while I turned right. I kept an eye on the kid as they headed down the run ahead of me. Both skied with the lithe grace of long-term skiers who could pick up the flow of the slope and the fall line with the greatest of ease. I stopped in front of twin scrawny, snow-encrusted Doug fir trees, the front one with the top freshly snapped out of it in the last winter storm, to watch Thomas and Mrs. K as they approached the terrain park.

Mrs. K avoided the first rail but stopped downslope from it. The kid did a 180 and started skiing switch, gliding backward down the black diamond slope without a pause, glancing back to keep track of the rail. He rode the rail gracefully, then dismounted with another 180 and raced after Mrs. K.

I shook my head and prepared to follow them down the easier slope that angled off next to the terrain park. Jesus the ski instructor. Heard a lot from kids, but that? Mountain kids learned to ski quickly, especially if they had any athletic talent.

The faint scrape of metal edge on snow followed by a surprised warning yelp startled me. I looked up and saw a big burly man careening in my direction, skis fixed in a snowplow wedge, sliding downhill far too fast for an easy stop. Before I could move away from the tree, he hit me hard, sending me flying onto the sharp points of the broken tree. My head slammed into its twin, and I had enough time to regret not wearing a helmet before I blacked out.

❀

It hurt like hell when I woke up, lying on the snow next to the trees. The guy bending over me wore a red jacket—instructor jacket or ski patrol, I wasn't sure which. Ice was forming on his short reddish-brown hair and his beard from the light snowfall.

"Are you all right?" he asked, and I realized I'd heard him repeating that question for several moments before I was actually conscious enough to register what he was saying. The night ski lighting seemed to create a halo around his head. "Are you all right?" he repeated.

"I hurt," I said. "Hit my head on that tree and landed on those splinters." I waved a hand somewhere toward where I thought the tree might be. Somehow, it didn't hurt as bad to move as I thought it might.

He rested a hand on my head, and it seemed to feel better.

"He gonna be okay?" That was a harsher voice, rather like the panicked yell from the guy who'd clobbered me.

"You got away with it, Pete. *This* time," the red jacket guy said.

"J.C., look, you promised me this would work!" Pete blubbered. "I didn't want to hurt anyone."

"I said it would work if you listened to me and did what I told you to do," J.C. countered. "But no, you had to go and try *this* slope, see if you had a hand for tricking. I *told* you it wasn't clear."

"Didn't think it was *that* hard," Pete muttered.

"Yeah, and wasn't that what you said about crucifixion?"

Pete grumbled and pushed up beside J.C. to look down at me. "Look, man, I'm sorry. I miscalculated. You going to be okay? What's your name?"

"His name's Casey," J.C. said.

My head was feeling better but I wasn't quite sure I was hearing some of what they said correctly. I must have really rung my chimes when my head clobbered that trunk.

"I think so," I said slowly. I wiggled fingers, toes, and legs. All there. I ran my hands up and down my sides, surprised that my parka wasn't ripped and that I didn't have long pieces of wood sticking out of my right side. I did remember hitting those splinters, and a faint soreness where I'd hit suggested I'd remember it more tomorrow.

J.C. ran his fingers along my neck, then down my chest. "A few aches and pains, but nothing big. Don't think we need to call for a backboard—good thing, Pete. Be hard to explain what we're doing over on this run, because I'm not supposed to bring beginners over here. Why don't you get Casey's equipment, and I'll put him back on his feet?"

Pete muttered assent, and J.C. turned to me. I blinked as he helped me sit up. Now I could see the name plaque on his coat—J.C., no further details. He still seemed to have a fuzzy halo around his head.

Pieces started to come together. *Pete.* I looked over at the burly guy gathering up my skis, shaking his head mournfully as he looked down at one bent and twisted pole, and a ski woefully out of camber. He had that faint glow about his head as well. Gloves conveniently covered up any marks that might be on J.C.'s hands, though, and his hair was long enough to cover up any marks on his head. I began to doubt again.

"Up on the count of three," J.C. said. "One—two—three!" He eased me up, with less effort than I thought.

Pete trudged up. "Dude, his skis are wrecked." He offered up the ski bent the wrong way, along with the bent pole.

J.C. made an annoyed sound and took the bent ski.

"Pete, all it takes is a little twist and this stuff goes back into shape. It's not rocket science." He started to turn away from me.

"You taught that kid to ski, didn't you?" I blurted. "Thomas. He said Jesus taught him how to ski."

Pete raised a brow at J.C. "Thought you were going incognito, J.C."

J.C. scowled. "You know how kids are. Even hormonal, pubescent males with an eye for the girls. Can't fool any of them. He guessed it right away."

"The Old Man won't like it. You're not supposed to be coming back."

J.C. shrugged and handed me my straightened ski, which looked better than ever. "He's got his own shady history of sneaking down here and talking to folks in the desert all the time. We've got an agreement about me and skiing."

"Kids." But Pete was grinning wide, even as he shook his head.

J.C. snorted and made no further pretense of what he was doing as he ran his hand down my pole. "There you are, Casey, your equipment's all fixed, you're all fixed, everything's been made right. Consider it a little local anomaly for your troubles."

"Thank you," I said. "But hey—any chance I can sneak in a lesson?" After all, if Jesus himself was a ski instructor, what kind of lesson could he be teaching? As a self-respecting ski bum, I wasn't going to pass up the chance.

Pete grinned at J.C. "Gonna do it?"

J.C. shook his head ruefully. "The things I do. Sure, why not? One of you to get down this slope, two of you, what's the difference?"

Pete laughed, and went to get his skis. J.C. and I snapped back into our skis.

At first the lesson was no different from any other I'd done. J.C. took us through the drills—poles lying vertical across our palms, facing our upper bodies downhill no matter which way we turned our hips and lower bodies. Then we whipped through the higher-level drills, weight changes, quickly moving into pole plants and the next level of techniques.

Pete improved quickly from the rank beginner who'd caused a wreck into a passable intermediate skier capable of taking on the black diamond runs at Treetop. My skills didn't pick up quite as quickly as Pete's but I still wasn't looking too bad. For once I could feel the fall lines and how they flowed down the slope. The three of us fell into a smooth, rhythmic pattern as we played with gravity down the steepest lines we could find on the lit runs.

"This is addicting," Pete panted at the top of one bowl that we'd hiked up, to find some unmarked snow. It was only slightly off of the beaten path. Even though this particular bowl wasn't lit, the light reflections off of the low hanging clouds gave us enough light to see our way down.

J.C. grinned at him. "Best invention yet, hmm?"

"Beats fishing the Dead Sea or shepherding in the desert any day. Gonna have to go talk to those Norse about this one. Sometimes those pagans come up with a good idea."

I laughed and pushed off first.

About halfway down this bowl, suddenly the snow around me started to move. I tried to pick up the pace to beat the avalanche, but it caught me, spilling past me at waist level before it sent me tumbling down the slope in a flood of white. I couldn't tell what was up or down as the current of snow rolled me around. One of my skis popped off and I lost track of my poles. I kept my hands in front of my face, trying to swim through the snow crystals, fighting to keep a breathing space clear.

At last I came to a stop. I tried to move my arms and legs. Nothing. It was as if I were cast in icy cement. I could just barely move my hands.

So this is how it ends.

I clawed at the snow around me, enlarging my breathing space. If I were lucky, I'd only be a few inches under. As I worked, I was able to free my arms and work them above my head—not that that was any guarantee as to which end was up. For all I knew, I could be digging down rather than up.

Cold seeped through me. I wasn't wearing an avalanche transponder. I hadn't planned on skiing anywhere near possible avalanche sites. Yeah, I was skiing with J.C. and Pete, but who knew if they'd be able to find me? Or even— and this possibility struck me as I lay in the growing white cold—if it had all been a figment of my imagination? After all, I did have days when I could ski almost this well on my own.

What a stupid move.

On top of everything else, I started getting sleepy. Until now I hadn't realized how tired I was getting. It was just the rhythm of a good night's skiing. But now, my side ached, my head hurt, and the pain wasn't enough to distract me from the growing drowsiness.

At last I decided to start murmuring a Rosary. Not much else to do. I went through several decades before my eyelids drooped, and my lips became heavy. At this point, the white stillness was mesmerizing. White was the color of death, I decided, not black. And a white death seemed oddly comforting and satisfying.

I accepted the white, and passed under its curtain. Maybe I'd find out if tonight had been a dream, up until the avalanche.

Maybe not.

⁂

I woke coughing and choking, and colder than the deepest frozen depths of Hell. J.C.'s hands on my shoulders were warm, and Pete's hands on my legs were almost as warm.

"Touch and go there," Pete said to J.C.

"It's not his time," J.C. said. "You with us now, Casey?"

I nodded, not wanting to admit to the doubts that had crossed my mind.

Pete laughed softly. "Don't worry about it, Casey. Everybody doubts now and then. You're looking at the king of second thoughts."

"We didn't find your stuff," J.C. said. "But we'll replace it for you."

I shook my head. "Guys, the experience has been just enough. But now, I think I've had it."

"Enough for one night," Pete agreed.

Between the two of them, they got me down to the bottom. It didn't take much persuading for the three of us to go into the bar and have a round of nachos and microbrews. Pete and J.C. fed me up, got me drunk, and poured me into my bed at the inn.

Next morning, I woke slowly. I hurt a little bit, certainly not as much as I should have. And, miracle of miracles, I didn't have the hangover I should have had with the number of beers we'd knocked back the night before. I *thought* that the microbrew had tasted a bit better than usual.

But I sighed. I'd gotten rather fond of those skis. They'd taken me past the rank beginner stage up to a semi-confident intermediate who could tiptoe out on the easier blacks. And now—well, they were buried under the snow somewhere up in that anonymous bowl, and probably weren't in skiable shape. I had several days of vacation left, but my budget sure didn't allow for buying a new pair of skis.

I dragged myself out of bed. Then something caught my eye.

Two pairs of skis rather like the ones J.C. and Pete had been riding last night leaned against the wall. I checked them out, stroking the topsheets, checking out the bindings. One was a nice pair of twintips, just what I needed to try out tricking. The other was a nice pair of all mountain fat skis, perfect for regular skiing. My size. I checked the DIN settings on the bindings. My setting.

Then I spotted the note on the table. I picked it up, noting the vaguely Hebraic style of the print.

Just a little something to make up for losing your own last night. Good riding. J.C.

I half-grinned.

Below that, in a rougher hand—

Don't do anything I wouldn't do.

Pete hadn't signed, but I knew who it was.

I laughed, and went off to breakfast with a lighter heart. Maybe I'd get lucky and run into them again. But if not— well, it had been worth it.

Thomas and Mrs. K sat at a table by the window, looking out on the street below, as I helped myself to the lavish continental breakfast our inn offered. Thomas looked away from Mrs. K, and our eyes met. We studied each other for a moment, and then he grinned and gave me a two-fingered wave before turning back to Mrs. K. I waved back at him, then found a seat on my own, studying the slopes above the street.

It was, after all, another good ski day.

"J.C. THE SKI BUM" had its origins in one of the Friday night ski events sponsored by the middle school where I was teaching. It was one of those bluebird ski nights, where there was just enough fog to diffuse the ski run lights, and I had gotten good enough to ski the challenging night run. After making a pass through there with another teacher, we rode up on the lift with a former student.

He was joking around and made the comment "Jesus taught me how to ski."

Needless to say, we didn't believe him.

But it did make the nice seed for a story.

2

THE WISDOM OF ROBINS

"I don't know why you had to build a nest *here*, Nora!" my partner Nick squawked. "So noisy. And all those two-leggeds walking by our nursery and staring at our children!"

"It's good access to food." I dove for a worm in the cultivated grass next to the rough area where I'd built our nest, in between two pathways the humans preferred. "And you'll thank me when Junior One or Two win the Summer Singoff."

"MA!" Junior One brayed, hopping toward me. "Gimme! Starving!"

I stuffed the worm down his craw to prove my point.

"You are right about food," Nick conceded, grabbing a bug three hops away from me. Junior Two cheeped at him and he gave the bug to Two. "But neither One nor Two have started a full song—and we've only got a few more days left before the Singoff."

"It will happen," I said with a confidence I didn't quite feel. All the singing from the humans in the camp. The chanting. And yet our latest clutch was delaying their song.

Not like last year's second clutch, who started singing complex verses even before the spots had faded off their chests.

"Hope you're right." Nick clacked his beak and hopped away. He grabbed at a huge night crawler. Junior One and Two mobbed him.

I snapped up a beetle all for myself. Song was a sore point for Nick. He had ambitions of elevating himself within robin society...but he lacked the song quality to achieve his goals, even though he had the nicest plumage of any of our flock's males.

But Nick was a good provider, even if he was a bit impaired on the song front. Our children were plump, well-feathered, and occasionally dominant singers. Nick grumbled at times about my opinions, but he usually supported me—especially after our second clutch did so well once I discovered this camp last summer and moved our nest here. And his feathers...oh, between his plumage and his attentive parenting—well, there was no other partner for me.

"Mama?" Grace, one of my daughters from the first clutch, hopped near. "Do you think the new two-foots will be as noisy as the last batch?"

"Humans can do funny noises with their noisemakers," I admitted. This last camp had featured metal things that blared and blasted but could also croon and warble. "But I think this one is different. No big funny-shaped containers. I think...it reminds me of the speakers from last year. They make music in rhythm and beats. Their regular noise, not their song sounds."

I hoped this was the case. Maybe exposure to rhythm and beats and not metal human sound was what Junior One and Two needed. This speaking gathering had been my first camp last year with our second clutch, born later than this batch. But still...the influence had shown up at the Singoff. Our first clutch, fledged higher in the woods and farther away from human influence, had performed like all our babies did. High scores on their plumage, moderately skilled singers, but not strong enough to be dominant, just like their father. I'd earned a pitying cheep from Maria, partner to Rob, the current Head Robin, after they had performed.

"Too bad your children take after their father's song and not your family," she'd said, ruffling her feathers and giving me the superior eye. Oh well. She was just jealous. Rob's plumage wasn't as beautiful and smooth as Nick's.

Then our third son beat Maria and Rob's Three in the Summer Singoff and it was my turn to give Maria a pitying cheep. He came in second overall, beating older males, and earned the name Red. Not quite Rob or Robin—and a first-year wouldn't be enough to challenge our Rob for flock leadership—but he performed well enough that Rob quietly suggested he seek a future mate and territory to rule in the lowlands.

This year I moved our nest even closer to human activities at the camp. Our first clutch was all girls, mostly raised by the time the humans started showing up at the camp, though they still roosted with Nick and now the new fledglings. But this second clutch? Two boys and a girl, all raised to the notes of human song and music. They also had taken to foraging around the camp lawns and listening to the humans. Their older sisters' private songs had changed, and it was my hope that I would see their nests around the camp as well next year—if they survived to find mates.

"Listen and learn from the people," I now said to Grace.

"Copy their rhythms and patterns in your song. Your children will learn from you and them."

"You'd think we would see it by now," Nick grumbled, hopping over to us.

"We still have a few days."

"TWEETSQUAWK!" Junior One screeched. "Tweet, tweetsquawk, TWEETSQUAWK."

Grace winced, and I wondered if One would ever get it together for the Summer Singoff.

Oh well. We still had Two as a family competitor.

And both One and Two still had their breast spots, though Two's were fading. They were young—wouldn't that count for something?

Several days passed. Junior Two took to hanging out by the outdoor human feeding station, almost overnight developing a fascination for the ants and bugs he found at the edge of the pavers. But he was silent in comparison to Junior One, who continued to squawk at me and Nick.

Occasionally, I thought I heard soft song from Two. The rhythm seemed to match that of one of the poets who made human words flow like song even though he wasn't singing. He bobbed up and down almost like he was dancing, fluttering his wings. It was different—but was it something that could win?

"Why don't you let me hear your song?" I asked him two days before the Singoff.

"Not quite ready yet." Before I could say any more the poet came outside, followed by a group of human fledglings. Two flew after them.

"I don't know about this." Nick landed beside me. "One is still squawking and Two—I've not heard him sing yet."

"He's practicing." I clacked my beak in frustration. "But I just asked to hear his song and he said he wasn't ready yet."

"His spots are fading faster than One's."

"I know." I pecked at an imaginary bug. Maybe Red's win last year had been a fluke. Maybe building a nest here wasn't as good as I thought it would be.

Nick fluffed up, then settled his feathers. "Just two more days."

"A lot can happen in that time."

"I hope you're right."

So did I.

We held the Summer Singoff up in the mountains, away from human activity. Nick led this year's family group, the girls from our first clutch right after him, then the second clutch behind them. I followed to make sure no one got lost or left behind.

When we reached the high mountain clearing, our family split off into appropriate groups—Nick to adult males, One and Two to second-clutch males, me and the girls to our own groups.

I won in adult females for song and feather condition. Grace earned second in first-clutch females for her song— her range surprised me, but she had ruffled a single wing-tip feather which disqualified her for feather competition.

But we all wondered about the male Singoff. The whole flock gathered in the aspen grove in the middle of the meadow, as Rob took position on a prominent limb.

"Maria, who are our female winners—and do we have a Singoff from your side?"

"Nora clearly won for both adult song and feathers," she reported, flicking her tail dismissively. "Jeanie from Charles and Karen won first clutch for song and feathers; Grace from Nick and Nora won song but was disqualified for feather condition for second overall. Second clutch—"

I missed the rest of her report as I glanced over at Nick. One and Two perched next to him, but I couldn't tell what the results were.

"Good job," Rob chirped, getting my attention back. "We have a Singoff for the males." He preened. "I won for the adults. Maria and my First One won first clutch for song and feather condition. Second clutch—" he paused. "It was a close competition. We have an *unusual* tie for first place, balanced by the feather condition of one of the competitors. The choices are Maria and my Second One, and Nick and Nora's Two. Both are excellent singers, but Nick and Nora's Two does not have as mature a feathering."

"Because he's *younger*," I peeped.

Rob nodded at me. "So age allowance makes the difference. I have no doubt that in two weeks his feathering will show the usual excellence we expect from Nick and Nora." He bowed to our Red, his second-in-command. "Judging is now based on song alone, for the first-years to earn the names of Rob and Red. Red, will you announce our contestants?"

I blinked hard. Three competitors. Two might be another Red...but I had hopes for more. If he won the name Rob, then he would lead the second-year flock adjacent to ours, with rights to challenge our Rob in the Spring Singoff. But if he were another Red...like last year's Red, I wouldn't see him after wintering.

I didn't think he could lose to Rob and Maria's First One and Second One.

Still, it was the Singoff, and one never knew.

"Rob and Maria's First One," Red announced.

Their First One perched next to Red. He began the ambitious, full-voiced finalist spring song, adding in a few extra warbles. A beautiful song, almost rich enough to be the song of a mature adult. Then, as he pushed his volume, a loud SQUAWK worthy of our One's TWEETSQUAWK emitted from his beak as his voice broke on a high, trilling note. The remainder of his song lacked the boldness of his start, occasionally breaking into a shrill, off-key tone.

One down, I thought. A possible Red—depending on how his brother and Two performed.

"Rob and Maria's Second One," Red proclaimed.

Second One began with less confidence than First One, though his voice also had the fullness of a mature adult. His notes were correct, but lacked the fluid beauty of First One's before his voice broke, nailing each one but not linking them. His chest was spotless and his plumage smooth and gorgeous. He finished smoothly, no squawks or off-key sounds. But his song was mechanical and precise, not ambitious. If Two also turned in a good song, then Second One might be a Red.

Come on, Two, I thought.

"Nick and Nora's Two."

Two flew to the main perch. He was bigger than his competitors but his chest still bore spots, clearly younger than they were. He ruffled and then smoothed his feathers. Then he started bobbing his head in a rhythmic beat, a one-two-THREE, one-two-THREE, fluttering his wings in syncopation.

Two started on a higher note than his competitors, fluttering his wings and bobbing his head as he slurred the notes of his morning song to match the beat. His voice was higher-pitched than the others, but instead of forcing a more mature volume and richness he worked on a more ambitious pacing than they used. When the notes became more difficult he slowed the pacing but it was still fluid, still smoother than Second One's.

At last he finished with a final bob and flutter, every note sung correctly.

"Now we vote. First One."

A few chirps. First One would be neither Red nor Rob for the second-year flock.

"Second One."

More chirps. But the majority of the flock remained silent—could it be?

"Two."

The clearing erupted in chirps and tweets. Rob glided over to join Red.

"The flock has spoken," he pronounced. "Nick and Nora's Two has earned the name of Rob for the first-years. Maria's and my Second One is the Red for that flock." He glanced over at our new young Rob. "Unless, of course, you would choose to seek prominence in a larger lowland flock."

The same thing he had said to Three last year.

Two—now First-Year-Rob—fluffed his feathers and sat up taller.

"I don't think so," he answered. "I am a mountain robin. Besides—" he glanced over at me. "I think I still have more to learn about song, and the mountains are the place to be for that."

Rob fluttered his feathers. "We shall see about that," he said, fixing First-Year-Rob with a stern gaze.

And even though our little Two still had a spotty breast, he preened before giving Rob a confident look in response. "So we shall," he said.

I busied myself with preening to keep from chittering with laughter.

Deep inside, though, I was exulting, a silent joyful song echoing through my thoughts. As I straightened back up, I saw Nick puffed up with pride. As Rob and Red continued to speak to the new First-Year Rob and Red, I flew over to Nick.

"So was I right?" I asked him.

"Nora Robin, you are very wise to have found such a good nesting site," he answered. "Let us hope that our son shares your wisdom."

"Given his choice—I think he does."

His voice lowered. "This time next year we might be Mother and Father of Rob. Dare we hope?"

"We'll know when the time comes."

But I was already dreaming of the prospect.

"The Wisdom of Robins" was written for the Whimsical Beasts CampCon anthology, and was roughly based on my observation of some fledging robins at the Summer Fishtrap writers' conference at Wallowa Lake.

3

VAMPIRE HUNTER VACATION

"Look! Cati! That's gotta be him!" Kerry whispered.

"Him *who*?" Cati glanced around, trying to figure out just who on earth Kerry was obsessing about *this* time.

"Dang it, took you too long to notice! The big guy. The one we were looking for. He went into the art gallery there." Kerry pointed to what looked like an old bank building.

Cati sighed. "Kerry, we're *on vacation*." Her Hunter senses couldn't pick up anything supernatural on the street crowded with lean, tanned, athletic men and women.

"Not if we stumble across a vampire."

"Here? Really?" Cati waved a hand toward the street. "Just look around. Is this a place where a vampire is going to hang out?" The tans sported by everyone on the street ought to rule out any of the vampires they were hunting.

If they were hunting vampires. Right now, they were on vacation, and Cati hoped to keep it that way. She had picked Labor Day weekend in Hood River for just that reason. No vamps, not likely to be any vamps, she'd think a pale-skinned vampire would stand out in an outdoor sports-oriented place like Hood River. Especially during the height of windsurfing season.

A perfect vacation for Kerry and Cati, vampire hunters.

But Kerry seemed to have found the exception. Kerry elbowed Cati. "Just what they told us about. The big guy, king of all the Oregon vamps. Mr. Shadow. Can't you feel him?"

"We're on vacation. I'm trying my best *not* to feel anything," Cati grumbled. "That's why I brought us here, to get some time off. What vampire worth his fangs is going to hang out someplace where everyone's biking, boarding, or doing something on the rivers or mountains?"

Kerry smirked at Cati. "You forgot about the arts and wine scene."

Cati made a face. "Like any vamp is going to be working in a winery."

"Art gallery. Like the one Mr. Shadow just disappeared into."

"You *are* going to make me work, aren't you?" Cati sprawled on the bench made out of windsurfing boards in front of the surf shop and pulled out her smartphone, tapping up her vampire detection app. She pressed the *Search* button, slowly rotating the phone from side-to-side, half-expecting the sensors to remain quiet.

Chime.

Cati looked up from her phone to see where the app pointed. The pulsing red arrow aimed up the street, toward the white stone building with two Ionic pillars framing the doorway that Kerry had indicated.

Gallery Edges, the sign strung between the pillars read. A reader board advertised wine tasting and tapas—and now Cati felt a sense of vampire nearby. Strong enough to be Mr. Shadow.

"What's *he* doing here? There aren't supposed to be vampires in this place. Too hot, too sunny."

"Selling art." Kerry shrugged. "Or being art. He's vain. What else? Let's go check."

Cati groaned, but followed Kerry across the street.

The gallery didn't look like any building she'd expect a vampire to hide in, especially the cautious, elusive Mr. Shadow. The east wall was made up of five windows extending two stories high, letting more light into the room than any self-respecting vampire would tolerate.

Then again, Mr. Shadow is strong enough not to mind the sun.

So far, however, he hadn't shown much interest in moving beyond traditional vampire behavior. Did this appearance indicate a change in strategy?

The gallery *was* unusually quiet for a Labor Day Weekend. A tall man in a blue shirt and black jeans stood behind a granite-topped bar and poured wine for two elegantly casually dressed women. Cati studied the three of them. None looked like vampire or vampire companions.

Need to keep this low-key, then. Don't want to freak the civilians.

"Doesn't look like he's on this floor," Cati murmured, looking around. The modernistic style of most of the art displayed didn't quite appeal to her.

Kerry jerked her head toward the stairs. "Up there. God, do I have to tell you *everything*?"

"I want wine first," Cati insisted, walking toward the bar. After all, it was a vacation, and a little wine wouldn't impair her ability to track down Mr. Shadow.

"You're delaying." But Kerry followed her.

Cati stopped. "Also helps us make sure those three are

non-affiliated. If they aren't, then we're good to go. Unless you want to get in their faces about it?"

"Heavens, no."

"Besides, a single glass of wine will relax us. White wine," Cati said to the bartender.

"One or two?" he asked.

Cati put her smartphone down on the bar, activating her vampire hunting app again, watching to see if he reacted. She raised her right eyebrow to question Kerry.

"Two," Kerry said. She stepped up to the bar.

Satisfied with the bartender's lack of reaction to her screen, Cati took her wine and checked the scanner. It pulsed pale red.

Vampire 20-40 feet away.

Vampire-marked nearby? Cati typed into the phone.

No.

Kerry finished her drink while Cati continued to study her app, turning her back to the bar and leaning against it. She sipped her wine, trying to get a sharper focus on the vampire.

"Come on, will you?" Kerry fretted.

The best she could get the app to do was to indicate that the vampire was upstairs. Cati drained her glass.

I so did not want to hunt vampires. This is supposed to be a vacation.

But if a vampire showed up, she was required to do something about it. And if this were actually Mr. Shadow, then....

"He's upstairs," she muttered to Kerry. "You want to do the honors?"

"It's your turn, and besides, I sensed him," Kerry whispered back. "You do it."

"All right." Cati bit back a groan. She was tired of hunting vampires.

It's your job, she reminded herself. *Your talent.*

But the talent that had seemed so exciting and challenging three years ago now felt like sheer drudgery.

Watch out. This stage is when most vampire hunters become prey.

That was one reason why Cati now hunted with Kerry. Training newer hunters kept old-timers from becoming complacent—and at three years, Cati was one of the oldest vampire hunters still working.

I just wanted a vacation....

As she reached the top step of the stairway her senses went on high alert.

Here.

She spotted the intricately worked brass crown sitting on an industrial drum.

His crown.

Cati had only seen Mr. Shadow with his crown once, in a big battle, and she wasn't about to forget it.

Above the crown hung two Day of the Dead masks. Cati eyed them. The design didn't quite look right—the lines flowed differently. Cati looked closer. Were the canines of the skulls' teeth sharper and pointed, like a vampire's would be? Yes. And did the teardrops on the masks take the shape of daggers interwoven with contorted tree branches, mirroring the shapes in the crown?

Yes.

"It's *him,*" Kerry breathed.

"It's his crown, anyway. Where is he?" Cati pretended to take a picture of the crown with her phone while holding her hand over it. She felt the power—but it slept.

Wake, she whispered to the crown in the Old Speech. As

the crown's power stirred, the Day of the Dead masks stirred and flowed into the shape of Mr. Shadow.

"Screen, Kerry!" Cati punched the button that activated her phone's vampire stealth-killing mode, and pointed her phone's camera toward Mr. Shadow. Kerry copied her.

Mr. Shadow snarled. *What are you doing here?* he thought at Cati, before she could punch the button again to finish him.

What are you *doing here?* Cati thought back. *I'm on vacation! You're not supposed to be in a place like this!*

Neither are you, Mr. Shadow answered, a petulant tone in his mind speech. *It's my vacation too! Stupid vampire hunters, being where they aren't supposed to be—*

Before she could push the button, Mr. Shadow faded away in a black swirl, darting toward the ceiling and disappearing. Cati and Kerry lunged for the masks as they fell toward the floor. They caught the masks and gingerly put them back.

"Did anyone notice?" Cati asked.

Kerry walked over to the balcony railing and looked over, then came back. "Not this time," Kerry said. "But Mr. Shadow took off."

"Fine by me," Cati said. "I want a vacation from vampire hunting. At least this week. I got the impression that Mr. Shadow feels the same way about being hunted."

"Maybe we should track him down?" Kerry suggested. "Find out what he's doing here."

"We are *on vacation*," Cati said. "As long as Mr. Shadow feels the same way and stays out of trouble, I fully intend to enjoy the rest of this week. It's up to him." She tapped in the appropriate code on her phone to drop the screen. "Unscreen," she said to it.

The man behind the bar gave them a suspicious look as

they walked out, but Cati didn't flinch one bit. He hadn't seen anything and he wasn't going to see anything.

She did have to wonder just what kind of vacation Mr. Shadow was contemplating.

"We probably should scan the town," Kerry said. "Just to be safe. If Mr. Shadow is feeding on someone we'll need to intervene."

"Doesn't mean we can't have fun at the same time." Cati checked her app. "App says he's at full power, so it's not likely he'll be looking to feed any time soon."

"Then why is he *here?*"

"Maybe he likes to windsurf." Cati shrugged. "Or bike. We'll need to check out the local activities. Just to be sure he's being a good boy."

"Oh, that's going to be *so hard,*" Kerry rolled her eyes and giggled.

"I'll let you take care of the sports on the river," Cati said. "Dibs on bicycling and hiking for me."

"And we'll *both* do the wineries."

"That's probably where we'll find him," Cati said.

Not that she wanted to find Mr. Shadow this week. His swift flight suggested that he didn't want to force a confrontation. Normally, Cati would ignore that and go after him.

But, like Mr. Shadow, she was ready for a vacation.

Wonder what will happen if we meet him at a winery?

The thought made her chuckle.

"What's so funny?" Kerry asked.

"Oh…just thinking about meeting Mr. Shadow at a wine tasting."

Kerry frowned. Then she giggled as well. "I'll bet you can't resist the temptation to tingle him just a little bit. Just to remind him that we're watching."

"I'll take that bet," Cati said, puffing herself up in feigned indignation. "I assure you that I have more self-control than that!"

"When it comes to Mr. Shadow? I'll have to see that."

"Just you wait," Cati said, looking around as she stood on the street corner. "I am on vacation!"

And no vampire is going to spoil that! Or, she amended her thought, *if he wants to push my boundaries, Mr. Shadow will find out just how annoyed I can be.*

But she didn't think he would.

Maybe vampires needed vacations as much as vampire hunters did.

A FEW YEARS BACK, *I participated in a mixed painting and writing Plein Air event based in Hood River.*

(Note: Plein Air = "a style of painting produced out of doors in natural light" or "taking place outside.")

So how does Plein Air work for writers? you might ask. After all, we can see what artists do. What do writers do when writing in a plein air style—if there can be such a thing?

Basically, we—writers and painters alike—went to the same location each day. The painters painted and the writers... wrote. Some wrote poetry, others meditations, and still others wrote stories.

"Vampire Hunter Vacation" is based on a sketch I wrote in downtown Hood River during that Plein Air event.

TRANSFORMATIONS

4

BREAKTHROUGH

The prehistoric GAWK-GAWK-GAWK of a blue heron roused from its rest echoed over the river as the summer sunset reflected yellow and orange in the dark water's roiling surface currents. Trina leaned on the wooden handrail of the bike bridge over the Willamette River as the river wound through Eugene, watching the heron as she tapped her fingers to the rhythm of "LA Woman."

A bike screeched to a stop behind her.

"I've been looking for you." Patty leaned her bike against the bridge's concrete wall.

Trina exhaled. "I'm not wanting to be found."

"Jeb's a jerk." Patty fumbled in her pocket, bringing out a palm-sized leather pouch.

"It's not Jeb," Trina sighed. "It's Rick."

Patty produced a small metal pipe and a baggie and started breaking off small chunks of bud into the bowl. "What's Rick got to do with anything?"

"Rick told me that if Jeb doesn't back off from running for City Council, he'll tell the press what Jeb was really doing in 1969."

"That's *all*?" Patty scoffed.

"Do you even know what Jeb was really doing ten years ago?"

"He left town to avoid that subpoena," Patty said.

"More than that," Trina said. "Lots more. Bad enough that Jeb won't tell me."

"Jeb's got a lot of secrets, honey." Patty emptied the ashes into her hand and scattered them in the river below.

"When I tried to get him to talk, he got on the phone to Rick instead."

Patty stuffed the pouch back into her jeans pocket. "So? Some'll see Jeb as a hero, others as a betrayer."

"I wish it was something that simple. No. It's like—he couldn't tell me. Couldn't make sounds come out of his mouth."

"*Jeb* not able to say anything?"

"Lips moving, not a sound. Made him madder than ever. And then he started dialing Rick."

Patty shook her head. "Weird."

They stared out over the river as the last wisps of light faded. The heron cried out again.

"Well, let's go back to the apartment. You're not going to get anywhere thinking about it *here*," Patty said.

"I guess not," Trina agreed.

They silently walked back to the apartment.

THE RECORD POPPED and snapped as it played "Break on Through," vying for primacy with "Barracuda" from the neighbor's stereo, as Trina helped Patty lug the bicycle up the single flight of stairs to their apartment. Their neighbor Karen stuck her head out the door as they passed.

"What's wrong with Jeb?" she shouted. "He's been playing that damn record over and over!"

Trina winced. "Barracuda" was Karen's cue that Jeb's stereo was too loud.

"I'll take care of it," she yelled back. "Sorry."

"Just get it turned down! I've got a headache."

"Sorry," Trina repeated.

She strode into the apartment. The tuner was cranked up as high as it could go. The sweet, rich scent of high-quality bud smoke oozed from the bedroom she and Jeb shared. Trina turned down the volume.

Jeb stomped out of the bedroom. "Why'd you turn it down?"

"Karen's got a headache!" Trina snapped.

Jeb shouldered past Trina to crank the stereo up again.

"Oh no you don't," Trina growled.

Jeb pushed Trina out of the way.

"I want it louder!"

"NO!"

They struggled. Jeb shoved Trina against the bricks and boards that held the stereo system. Her hand hit the turntable and the needle skittered across the vinyl.

"Damn it!" Jeb carefully replaced the arm on the rest. "It's scratched now! I won't be able to—damn you, Trina!" He turned on Trina, slapping her.

"Stop it!" Patty shoved in between them. "Stop it, Jeb!" She sent him sprawling. "Just what has gotten into you? You're not a hitter!"

Jeb lunged at Patty, growling incoherently. And then he stopped. Odd noises came out of his throat. His eyes widened as his face elongated along with his legs and arms.

He let out a squawk akin to the cry of the heron that Trina had heard earlier, then ran out the door.

Trina exchanged puzzled looks with Patty.

"What was *that*?" Patty said.

"I don't know," Trina said. "But maybe we ought to go find him."

"I think we'd better take care of you first."

"What do you mean?" Trina asked. "I'm fine. He didn't hurt me."

Patty slammed the apartment door shut and grabbed Trina's hand. "You'd better take a look at this." She dragged Trina in front of the bathroom mirror.

Trina stared at the reddish mark across her lips. Instead of fading like a normal slap mark, it had turned purplish. The area around the discoloration was rising, forming odd-shaped bumps that squirmed under her skin.

"Whisky Bar" started up on the turntable, more distorted than it had been before.

"He's back. Get that turned down before Karen calls the cops!" Trina croaked, finding it hard to force words past the tightness closing her throat.

Patty nodded and left.

Then Patty screamed.

Trina rushed to join her.

Jeb sprawled on the floor, face down.

Patty knelt beside Jeb. "He's—he's not breathing!"

Trina stared at Jeb's body, half-bird, half-man, barely able to concentrate for the *thing* moving in her face in time to the music.

The song ended. The turntable's arm lifted, spun back over to the armrest, then moved back to begin the record again. Trina raced over to the turntable and hit the stop button, but the machine kept going. She unplugged the turntable, stopping the record in the middle of "Break On Through."

The *thing* in her face stopped.

"Trina—" Patty repeated. "He's not breathing."

Trina grabbed Jeb's half-wings, half arms, and rolled him over onto his back. What remained of his face was twisted in fear, around the shape of a long, pointed, heron-like beak.

What— Trina started to say.

But a loud "rawk" came out of her mouth. Trina tried to scream, but another "rawk" escaped her lips. She fumbled to her feet, and stumbled toward the door. *Things* crawled and poked under her skin, her shape changing as she staggered outside. As she tripped down the stairway, feathers sprouted out of her fingers.

Rick stood at the bottom of the stairs, wrapped in darkness. He pointed at her, stopping Trina in place. Rick started to climb toward her.

"No!" she cried, but it came out as a third "rawk."

She couldn't wait. Trina crouched and spread her wings, then pushed off of the stairwell. Rick yelled curses at her as she flew past him and turned down the alley. Her first few strokes were weak and graceless, but as she gained altitude and tucked her long legs back under her tail, she gained strength and power.

The river. Safety was at the river.

Trina aimed toward the Willamette, following the pathway she and Patty had just taken from the bridge. She flew over the footbridge, angled down the river, and flopped into the trees. She crashed through branches before landing at the bottom of a tall cottonwood. Trina slowly regained her feet, and shook herself to realign her feathers. She looked up at the tree speculatively. Without words, she knew she needed to roost in it. But she knew it would be a challenge as a new flyer.

Instead, she tiptoed through the shallows of the river, and took up a stance on a rock. The rock fit her new feet perfectly, and it gave her some chance to see around her, even in the darkness.

The river's chattering, steady roar lulled her into uneasy sleep.

"WHA?" Trina sprawled into cold water. Her butt landed on a sharp river rock. Darkness surrounded her, but she was stark naked. How had she ended up in the middle of the river, with no clothes on?

As she clumsily found her feet amongst the river rocks, memory swept back. The fight with Jeb. His unexpected attack. His body—<u>no!</u>—and her own change. And Rick—

Trina clawed onto the riverbank and into a clump of brush, shaking with sobs. Jeb dead. His body changed. And the changes to her own body—*what happened?*

"Wha's that?" a male voice slurred. "Sounds like a girl."

"Cryin'," another male voice answered.

Trina stumbled to her feet.

"Maybe that girl whasshisname told us to find," the first man said. "Said she'd be around here somewhere."

Trina didn't dare wait. As she bolted from cover, one of the drunks was close enough she could smell the alcohol on his breath. He grabbed her arm and she hit him in the face. He fell back and she took off, grateful when a few strides brought her to the blacktopped bike path. She didn't stop to think about whether Rick—had to be Rick they were talking about, after all Jeb was dead—would be waiting for her along the path but simply ran as hard as she could.

A deeper darkness warned her as she neared the intersection with the footbridge. Trina skidded to a stop before the darkness noticed her and tried to still her gasps.

Darkness turned toward her before she could bolt again.

"Trina." Rick's voice was flat and dull.

"You killed Jeb," she said.

"No, I didn't. He made a mistake. Don't make the same one."

"What? Trusting you?" Trina wrapped her arms around herself. "I've never trusted you. And now—*this*—is happening to me—"

"Trina. Come to me. I'll make this work." Lawyerly persuasiveness reasserted itself in Rick's voice. "Jeb wasn't good for you. Too impulsive, too likely to take off for the woods without warning."

"That's what I loved about him!" Trina cried.

"You were infatuated with him." Rick came closer. "Why would you choose him over me?"

Because you're a lying scumbag, Trina thought. Aloud, she added, "Because you're not my type."

"You'll find I'm more your kind than you think." Rick took two steps toward Trina and she backed up.

"No," she breathed. "No."

"Stupid," Rick growled. "You don't have any clothes on. You don't have control of your changes. I bet you don't even know what triggers them. I can teach you."

Trina hesitated. Then she remembered Jeb's still body.

"Help me like you *helped* Jeb?" she asked. "No thanks!" She backed up two more steps. She could probably outrun Rick if she really tried. He didn't do anything to keep fit.

Rick screamed. The darkness surrounded Trina before she could flee.

Bird. I need to change into a bird. Then I could fly out. How do I do that? Maybe if she wished hard enough—*Doors music. Jeb was listening to The Doors. I wonder if that can trigger—*

Rick laughed. "If I can't have you, he can't either!"

"I'd much rather be dead with Jeb than live with you!"

"Who says Jeb's dead?"

"H-h-he—" Trina stammered. "He wasn't breathing?"

"Did you check any closer?" Rick's voice mocked.

"I was changing—"

Bicycle tires screeched to a stop on the footbridge above them.

"Patty!" Trina screamed.

A tall, lanky form tackled Rick. Suddenly they were surrounded by strains from the Grateful Dead, the bootleg tape Patty had made from the last concert she attended.

Rick finally lay still under his attacker. Jeb wobbled toward Trina.

"Crank it up higher!" he yelled back to Patty as the darkness tightened around Trina. "Hold on," he told Trina, and carefully reached into the darkness, singing along with the Dead. The darkness slowly faded away.

Trina dropped to her knees. Jeb picked her up.

"I—I thought you were dead!" she sobbed into his chest.

"The Dead counteracts the spell. Karen was playing it after Heart. That's what brought me back. How we were able to chase Rick off."

"Jeb, what's going on?"

"It's a long story," Jeb said quietly. "I'd like to get out of town before Rick wakes up. *We* need to get out of town."

Trina shivered, chills running up and down her body as Jeb carried her up the embankment. "Patty won't be safe either."

"Rick won't dare touch Patty," Jeb said. "Not a Deadhead." He put Trina down. Patty helped Trina get sweats and shoes on while Jeb steadied her. She couldn't stop shivering.

"Trina. Hop on behind me," Jeb said. "You're not going to want to walk to the apartment." He mounted the bike and held it steady as Patty helped Trina climb onto the seat. They pushed off, Jeb standing up as Trina held onto his waist.

Trina got off and walked beside Jeb when they got to Franklin Boulevard. Even at this late hour, Franklin was still busy. Something stirred the mixed flock of geese and ducks bedded down by the Millrace into honking and quacking. The birds settled back down as Jeb and Trina walked past the replica of the Willamette Meteorite and under the hulking edifice of the Science building.

"What happened with Rick?" Trina asked.

"It was a stupid mistake," Jeb said. "We'll talk later."

"I need to know."

"You will. This—isn't the best place to talk about it."

"When?"

"Anywhere but here. Let's get our butts out of town. Just trust me, okay, Trina?"

"I thought I could—until tonight," she said in a low voice.

"I'm sorry. God, Trina, I really am sorry I hit you. Never did that before, never will again. I was just—" Jeb sighed. "We have to get away from Rick's power over us. Now."

"Is this—Rick's power over us, our changes—going to be permanent?"

"I hope not. I have some ideas—but we can't do them here. We have to go where it first happened."

Back at the apartment, Trina dazedly helped Jeb throw clothing and camp gear into backpacks and stow it in his beat-up F-100 pickup. She boxed up food while Jeb loaded the cooler with everything except ice.

"We'll stop to get ice," he told Trina.

"How long will you be gone?" Patty asked.

"As long as it takes," Jeb told her. He wrote her a check. "This should cover our share of the rent. My turn this month."

Trina stirred. "I thought it was—"

"*My* turn," Jeb insisted. "It's the least I can do. We could be gone for a couple of weeks or more."

"What are you two going to do?"

"The less you know, the better," Jeb said. "Keep the Dead playing. Rick will be coming back around to find out where we've gone, and that's your best offense against him."

"So what *are* we doing?" Trina asked.

"Lifting the spell Rick created," Jeb said.

"Good luck, you two," Patty said, hugging Trina. She followed Trina and Jeb out to the green Ford pickup, and waved goodbye.

Trina fell asleep as they headed up the McKenzie River highway. She stirred when Jeb pulled over at the top of the Santiam Pass. They sat on the truck's tailgate while munching on sugary breakfast rolls and drank coffee from his Thermos. Light began to spread out in the forest around them.

Day grew stronger as they dropped down off the crest of the Cascades and into the ponderosa pine forest of the east side. Trina fell asleep before they reached Sisters. The truck bouncing on rutted roads woke her with a start.

"Where are we?" she asked Jeb. An antelope herd startled up in huge, bounding leaps as the truck drove by.

"Big Summit Prairie, in the Ochocos," Jeb answered. "There's a small prairie up higher that we'll hide out in."

"Will Rick be able to find us there?"

"Maybe. The place itself has a power, Trina. We should be safe."

"I hope you're right."

"If we're not safe there, we're not safe anywhere."

Jeb turned down a narrower road. She spotted more antelope and a few deer as they climbed higher, the road turning narrower and rougher. They passed several smaller prairies, the road following the edges of the open areas rather than plowing straight through the middle.

They turned onto a dirt road that followed the edge of one of the prairies, and yet again on a road that was barely more than two tiny ruts. Jeb pulled off the track and stopped in a small clearing at the edge of the prairie, surrounded by tall ponderosa pines and a small screen of lodgepole between the clearing and the prairie, with a rock circle in the middle.

"Here we are," Jeb said. "Antelope Prairie. We'll be able to see and hear anyone who drives this way, long before they can see us. This is where we'll break the spell."

Trina nodded. She and Jeb set up camp. After that, they went on a long hike, then collapsed on their bed inside the small backpack tent. Trina let the soft roar of the afternoon breeze lull her into sleep.

The shadows of afternoon were darkening into evening

as she woke. Jeb stood by the fire ring, staring out across the bitterbrush and grasses toward the treeline on the other side.

"Is something wrong?" she asked.

Jeb shook his head and put his arm around her. "Nothing. Now."

"Jeb, what's going on?"

"Rick wants control," Jeb said, sharply. "And he'll deal with the Devil himself if he could to get political power and control. He wants Eugene as his own personal playground."

"But the shapechanging—all that stuff?"

Jeb sighed. "Come on, let's get comfortable." He led her over to a fallen ponderosa trunk where they could watch the prairie. "We started playing around with some exotic drug he said came from a wizard chemist. LSD-plus, he called it. And underneath the influence—well, you saw what he became, and what I became. He's had power over me for the last ten years."

"But me? How?"

"I was trying to raise the change on my own. The Doors. Rick's always used that as a trigger. Create the change, then take an antidote to change back. When I told him I wasn't dancing to his game anymore, he kept the antidote from me. You—your connection to me—when I hit you, in the process of change, with our connection, that was just enough to transmit the ability to change to you." He frowned. "Trina, I swear to you. I've never been a hitter. I don't know what came over me then. I am sorry. So damned sorry."

"Just don't—don't do it again. Or I'm gone."

"If I hit you again," Jeb said grimly, "you've every right. I'm not a hitter. I don't know—"

"He tried to come on to me. He wants me for himself."

"He wants everything for himself," Jeb said.

"So what do we do now?"

"We wait," Jeb said. "We rest, and center ourselves."

"And then?"

"And then we raise the change. There is a way to stop the changes without the antidote. If we don't get interrupted before then. Rick *could* find us, but it'll take him several days before he can recover. By then—" His voice trailed off.

Trina shivered, suddenly cold despite the summer warmth.

THEY SLOWLY UNWOUND over the next few days. Trina got to know the birds around the camp; the liquid trill of the brilliantly blue mountain bluebirds that seemed to be tiny pieces of moving sky; the shrill call of the gray jays that sought to snatch food during their meals; the distant call of the ferruginous hawk that soared over the prairie; and the deep hoots of the owls around their camp. Every night there seemed to be more owl calls.

"Almost time," Jeb said one night, as they listened to the owls hooting while they sat around their tiny fire.

Trina shivered, dreading what was to come.

That night, she dreamed of flying high above the city at night. Unlike her first experience, she had control over her wings. Then she confronted a shadow, and, startled, spilled from the air, struggling to recapture that smooth pattern of flight. The strains of "Wild Child" thudded about her. Rick's laugh echoed in her ears while she spiraled toward the ground.

"Trina. Trina. Let it go. Let it go!"

She woke, thrashing in Jeb's arms. Her face felt twisted out of shape and her arms were still covered in feathers.

"Shh, Trina, shh," Jeb soothed. He began to sing roughly. As she recognized the tune of "Uncle Jon's Band," Trina sang with him, her voice still raucous and tuneless. As it steadied and mellowed, she felt her face change back and the feathers slowly disappear.

Once they finished, Trina burst into tears. "How do we stop this?"

Jeb kissed her forehead. "Tomorrow night," he said.

Trina woke late. She heard snatches of static-laded music from the alternative rock station out of Bend as she crawled out of the tent. Jeb stared into the heart of the prairie. She joined him and he pulled her close.

"Tonight," he said. "We need to rest as much as we can."

Jeb kept the radio playing all day. Neither of them ate. They sat by the tree line, watching the open prairie, the hawk, the bluebirds, the clouds skittering overhead, and the road at the far end of the prairie.

As dusk began to claim the prairie, Jeb rose. He silently stripped, then picked up a fallen ponderosa branch. Once she was naked, and had her own branch, Trina followed Jeb as he drew a large circle around their fire pit, careful to keep inside.

When the circle was completed, Jeb picked up two small baggies from beside the fire ring, one full of blue-colored salt, the other of red-colored salt. He handed the baggie of blue salt to Trina. She followed Jeb as he scattered the salt along the circle's line. When they were finished, Jeb took the baggies. He loaded a cassette into the boom box but did not start it. Instead, he stoked their small fire, then took Trina's hand and turned to face the trees. A single ray of fading sunlight broke through the clouds and briefly lit the campsite.

Then it was dark, except for the fire behind them.

Jeb took Trina into his arms, and kissed her. "Know this —whatever happens, I love you."

She nodded.

"Follow what I do. No matter what."

Jeb turned on the boom box. "Wild Child" poured out of the speakers. He began an arrhythmic, jerky dance that matched the opening chord sequence. Trina danced behind Jeb. With each phrase, she felt the change progress, until by the end of the song, both she and Jeb had completely changed form.

The first notes of "Riders on the Storm" rippled out from the boom box. Trina saw distant headlights and stopped. Jeb sounded a trilling call to regain her attention.

Follow what I do. No matter what happens. She turned her attention back to the dance, running in small steps behind Jeb, angling her wings like Jeb did, despite the flashes of headlight across the prairie and the distant sound of a car engine laboring as it turned onto the rougher track.

Follow what I do. Her legs suddenly shortened, and she flapped her wings to keep her balance as wings and body changed, the long beak dissolving back into her face. She flew behind Jeb, her Spotted Owl self smaller than his Great Gray.

Headlights blazed into their camp as the song ended. Jeb landed on the back of a chair. Trina landed on the other chair as Rick jumped out of his car, raising the cloud of darkness around him.

The strains of "LA Woman" blared from Rick's car.

Jeb hooted, then flapped his wings, rising from the chair back as Rick reeled to a stop at the edge of the circle, losing his balance and falling back. He yelled incoherent words at them. Trina followed as Jeb began to circle again, transforming into an eagle while she became a peregrine. This shape change was different, swifter, felt more in the way she flew than in the change of her body. The air around her became a friend that she could swim through with a lithe grace that caressed her falcon's body.

"LA Woman" segued into "Break on Through." Jeb used the rising thermal from their fire to climb higher, Trina underneath him. Then he banked to one side as Rick tried to step into the circle, smudging the salt. Rick was half-in, half-out of the circle as Jeb the eagle stooped hard on him and raked him with his talons. They whirled around Rick, striking him hard, sending him reeling inside the circle, spinning until he collapsed into the fire with a great wave of sparks. His body folded up, collapsed, and a whip-poor-will flew out of the flames and away from camp.

Jeb landed, Trina next to him, as the first strains of a Grateful Dead song she couldn't identify right away started. Slowly, she felt the change start.

Human. Again.

"Now what?" she asked Jeb. "How long before he finds his shape again?"

"He broke the circle," Jeb said. "It may never happen."

"What about this?" She gestured toward Rick's car. "Someone will look for him."

"We'll have to take care of it," Jeb said. "There's a cliff along the road." He pointed toward the road which ran through camp. "They'll see the tire tracks indicating he was here. We'll report it—he was drunk. Fought with me because he wanted to break us up. You told him no, and he took off in the dark. We followed, but he went off the cliff. Clean up the circle first, then we'll go—and take care of it."

Trina nodded as she dressed. "It'll still look suspicious."

"Rick has a reputation out here," Jeb muttered. "The good old boys don't take too well to Eugene frat boys who think they know it all. Without a body, there's not much to be done." He pulled on some gloves.

They broke camp in the dark. Jeb cleaned up the salt and put out the fire, then took Jeff's little MG.

Soon enough, the deed was done.

"Now what?" Trina asked Jeb, a yawn escaping her as the scenery around them began to grow light.

"We'd better talk to the sheriff," Jeb said.

Trina shivered.

"It'll be okay. You'll see," Jeb promised. "We're past the worst of it."

It took until dark for them to be finished with the sheriff. As Jeb promised, it went smoothly, and they checked into the small motel across the street from the courthouse rather than drive back to Eugene.

That night, she dreamed of flight.

When she woke, a single wingtip feather lay on the pillow next to her head. Jeb raised a brow at her, but said nothing. She thought she saw him slip a single feather into his bag, as well.

We are not done with those shapes.

She was surprised to find that thought oddly comforting.

W*HILE* I'*VE* W*RITTEN* *(and published) during different eras of my life, "Breakthrough" led off the resumption of my short story writing career. Jeff Dennis, who had published one of my short stories in an earlier era, approached me along with others to contribute a music-themed story somehow incorporating a nightbird.*

I had been processing some other events in my life, including a disastrous camping situation where we encountered drunken bow hunters. But I was also in the mood to draw on some of my history from my college years at the University of Oregon.

This is probably the only story which will touch on that side of my life...for various reasons.

5

ELECTORAL CHANGES

Molly Martinez's cell buzzed as she pulled up in front of Fellini's campaign office. She sighed as the caller ID came up. Reed McAllen. Former ally, sometimes lover, and the best damn campaign organizer in Woodville after herself. Why was he calling her first thing in the morning? Must be some juicy political gossip or he needed to vent. His candidate in the Congressional district next to Fellini's, Elena Karsten, was rich but a handful.

Thank God Fellini hired me before Karsten got around to making me an offer.

She tapped her earbud to connect.

"Hey Molly." Reed's voice was tight and nervous, not normal for him. "I've got a problem with Karsten. You're not gonna believe it. She changes shapes."

"What, so she's like a werewolf or something? Dude, you've gotta stop watching that scifi TV stuff. Rots your brain."

"Molly, I'm not kidding."

Molly sighed. "Reed, I don't have time for this."

"Molly, I'm worried. Really worried."

"It could just be your election nerves." Molly rolled down her window as a volunteer scurried toward her. "Tell Bob I'll be right in," she called. "Sorry," she said to Reed. "I'm getting swarmed."

"Me, too. Listen. This isn't election nerves. Molly, I *saw* the woman change shape. Literally. I swear."

She decided to play along. "How are you gonna keep this one from the media?"

"I'm—not worried about the media, Molly.

"Then what *are* you worried about?"

"You're gonna think I'm crazy."

"No more than usual."

Reed snorted. "Okay," he said. "Karsten looks just like a big spider when she changes. I'm afraid she's eaten a couple of people. Volunteers are missing—and from what I saw before the last one disappeared—from our headquarters—I'm scared. For myself. And I can't afford to drop her as a client. Child support. I need you to come see this. Her. I know we've only got three weeks left until the general, but—"

"I can't. If my candidate was sitting better in the polls, I could come on down. But Bob has his big City Club debate tomorrow, and if I'm not here to hold his hand—well, that's what he's paying me the big bucks for."

"I understand," Reed said.

"God, Reed, you know I'd do it if I could."

"I know." His voice went flat. "Sorry to bother you, Molly."

"Reed, it's not an issue of bother—"

"Later, Molly." He hung up.

"Damn it, Reed—" Molly glowered at her phone. The volunteer knocked on her car window again.

"Molly, Mr. Fellini's got a question for you about mass transit."

Molly sighed and slipped the cell phone into her pocket.

"Tell Bob everything he needs to know is in the white binder marked TRANSIT in the middle of his desk. I'll be right in."

I'll call Reed tonight, she decided.

"Ms. MARTINEZ?" The voice on Molly's cell that afternoon oozed a rich warmth that wanted to curl up around her ear and flow down her neck.

"Yes?" Molly bit back her surprise. The caller ID had shown Reed's number. "To whom am I speaking?"

"Karsten. Elena Karsten. You're an acquaintance of Reed McAllen."

"And you're his client. Ms. Karsten, what are you doing calling me from Reed's phone?"

"I have a problem," Elena Karsten said. "It seems Reed has gone missing."

Molly swallowed. "And you're calling me because—?"

"It's an inconvenient time to be without a campaign manager. I'm down by five in our last poll, and I need someone to take Mr. McAllen's place."

"Ms. Karsten, I'm contracted to manage Robert Fellini's campaign for Congress. I can't just jump from his Congressional campaign to yours."

"I think you'll find that Mr. Fellini will be very—cooperative—when you ask him to loan you to me."

"Ms. Karsten, I just can't—"

"You will. Talk to Bob."

The phone clicked off. Molly redialed, but it clicked

straight through to Reed's voice mail. A text chimed on her phone.

Fellini releases you, it read. *See you tonight.*

Molly growled and paced through the office to look for Fellini.

Reed, what kind of mess have you gotten me into now?

MOLLY SCOWLED as she squinted at the faded numbers above the storefronts, looking for Karsten's office. She spotted it at last, more decrepit and faded-looking than she would have expected from one of Reed's campaign offices. Even the lawn signs in the window looked faded and cobwebby.

"Molly Martinez," she said to the staffer at the front desk.

"Ms. Karsten is waiting for you." The staffer pointed toward the back. "Third door on the right."

Molly glanced around as she walked toward Karsten's office, but saw nothing to give her any hint about what might have happened to Reed. She knocked on the third door.

"Ms. Martinez. How nice to see you," Elena Karsten eased the door open.

"Yeah, well, let's hope this isn't a loss for my former client," Molly muttered. "I know Reed usually leaves pretty detailed notes about what he's been doing—updates his laptop just about hourly."

"He left his laptop here. I've got his passwords so I'll get it up and running for you."

That's not right, Molly thought. *Reed never goes anywhere without his laptop, and he never gives his passwords to a client.*

As she walked to Karsten's desk, she noticed the gargoyles posed along its edge.

"That's interesting," she said, picking one of them up. The face was almost life-like.

"Please don't touch those," Karsten snapped, looking over the top of her half-frame glasses.

Molly replaced it. She was about to turn to the laptop when she noticed the expression on the end one.

Reed's eyes moved as she looked at him.

"What the—" Molly leaned closer to study the Reed figure.

She startled back as Karsten changed form.

Reed was wrong, she had just enough time to think as she shrank, transforming into stone. *Medusa, not spider.*

Never reached this level when working on political campaigns, but I drew on that experience when drafting this story.

That said, I've never run into a candidate that literally turned campaign workers into stone, either.

6

RIVER-KISSED

Marthe paused at the Great River's edge. The cold spring flow delicately tickled her toes as dusk's shadows crept toward her. An anticipatory shudder ran through her lean, wiry body. The River rumbled solemnly by, the steady lapping of waves on the shore a soft, lulling chorus as evening unfolded.

Soon, she thought. *Soon I will change.*

The distant "ki-ki-ki" of a startled killdeer stirred Marthe into taking the first step into the River. Mud and sand billowed around her feet as she slid her feet along the bottom in measured, careful steps. The Great River had deep, treacherous drop offs.

The steady current flowed strong, tugging at Marthe's body as the waters swirled up to her crotch. Her next step found nothing but water beneath it. Marthe stopped. She pulled her foot back, seeking the edge. It was barely an inch in front of her standing leg.

Close.

Out here in the River, she could hear the mountain river she'd been dedicated to chuckle and roar its way into the

Great River. If she turned her eyes upstream, she could see its outflow.

Marthe didn't look. The river known as the Mountain's Child was her past. Her present and future lay with the Great River. She kept her eyes focused straight ahead, bracing against the tug of the River's current as it sought to drag her over the waiting edge. She pulled off her snug-fitting, embroidered turtleneck, revealing stringy arm muscles and flabby breasts that lay flat against her chest.

"To you, this gift, O River," Marthe whispered, and threw the shirt as far as she could out into the River. The current caught the turtleneck. Then, poof! It was gone.

"The River gives, the River takes," Marthe muttered through chattering teeth. "Blessed be the name of the River." She ran her fingers along her bare neck, fingering the gills developing under her skin. The skin moved under her fingers, but showed no sign of separating yet.

"The change will happen soon enough," she assured herself.

She squatted in the cold water until it pulsed against her chin. She stripped off the rest of her clothing, letting the River pull each piece from her fingers as she removed it. At last the only thing she wore was the medallion old Jehan the storekeeper had given her that morning, hanging from a slender black leather thong that seemed too light for the heavy silver disc.

The River lifted the medallion slightly off of Marthe's neck. She covered it with one hand as she faced west, watching the sun ooze behind the western hills.

At last the sun was gone, leaving only a faint golden glow in the sky. A matching glow came from her little fire above the waterline. Marthe sighed.

Done for tonight.

She stood and lost her balance, toppling into the water. The River pulled Marthe over the drop off. She mastered the brief surge of panic that washed over her as the waters closed over her head.

Can I breathe water yet? she wondered, holding her breath as the River pulled her down deep. But she didn't test her developing gills. If she breathed the water now, she'd be no different from any other person lost to the River, not one of the River-kissed kindred.

The current snatched at her medallion with watery fingers, lifting it off her neck.

No, Marthe thought. *Don't get greedy!*

The River chuckled.

Not yet, Marthe thought. *Not this time. Not this place. Be patient. Wait.*

The River sighed. The current holding Marthe eased. She kicked hard and her head broke the surface of the water, bobbing up a hundred yards downriver from her fire. The medallion settled against her chest as Marthe swam upriver, until her fingers and toes brushed against the sandy bottom.

"Not this time," Marthe said to the River. She gathered up driftwood on her way back to camp, and threw it on the fire all at once so that she could dry herself. Once dry, she rummaged in her pack for another pair of pants and a shirt. Then she ate jerky and dried fruit, washing it down with small mouthfuls of the pint of Old Overshoes she'd bought from Jehan that morning.

River-kissed, the River whispered to her in soft gurgles and lappings. *River-kissed. Come dance with me.*

"Not yet," Marthe said. She took one last fiery mouthful of Old Overshoes, tucked the bottle away, then settled her pack to use it as a pillow and crawled into her bedroll.

River-kissed, river-kissed, the River sang to her as she settled into sleep. *Be mine, oh river-kissed.*

"I ask for first night's protection," Marthe finally murmured.

The waves lapped strongly against the shore for four splashes, then eased back into their steady, quiet pattern.

Not yet for the dance, oh River-kissed, the River whispered. *But soon you will be mine.*

"Soon," Marthe agreed. "But not here. At Swedetown."

Not here, the River echoed. *But we will dance. Soon. At Swedetown.*

Marthe turned over and went to sleep.

Next morning, Marthe knelt by the ashes of her fire. She drizzled the last of her cooking oil over a handful of ashes. Then she used a fingertip to trace three wavy parallel lines, sign of the River-kissed, on her forehead and on each cheek.

Marthe waded back into the River and rinsed her hands. She checked her marks in the faint reflection of the River, pushing back her scraggly, colorless ash-blond hair from her face, scowling. She'd done better than this before.

"Out of practice," she said aloud. "Too quiet on the Mountain's Child."

Good enough for the City, River chuckled at her as he twined around her ankles. This morning he seemed playful, almost smaller and younger. He ran ten feet lower than the night before, revealing a strip of firm, damp sand.

Tide's going out, Marthe thought, marveling. She wouldn't see the great ocean, not unless her journey took her past Swedetown. But she had heard of the effect the ocean's tides had on the River even here, a hundred miles

56

inland from the ocean. She'd heard the tide effect lasted a hundred miles more upriver, all the way to the great falls that roared over the remnants of one of the mighty dams that had once tamed the River.

She trudged out of the water and up the bank. Her pack and bedroll waited by the exhausted fire. She tucked her boots inside her pack. Best to save them for later. On this bright, sunny morning, while walking next to the River, she'd go barefoot. The River provided a nice, sandy path.

A light upriver breeze stirred the River's smooth surface as Marthe shouldered her pack and began walking. Gulls glided around her, looking for food. Marthe ignored them, studying the broad, flat expanse of the River. It looked wider than she could swim easily, wide enough to swallow ten of the Mountain's Child without visible effect.

Her gull companions gave up and flew downriver, joining another pack squabbling over something at River's edge. Marthe squinted but she couldn't see what the attraction was. A great bald eagle dived toward the gulls. They complained loudly as they scattered. The eagle landed. It shook itself to settle its feathers, then marched toward what the gulls had found and began to peck at it.

Marthe ventured further up the bank. The eagle spread its wings protectively over its find, a huge spring salmon carcass, screeching as Marthe eased by. The gulls took advantage of her presence to harass the eagle until it took flight and chased them.

The gulls routed, the eagle cut in front of her, dropping a feather. Marthe stooped to pick it up, watching the eagle. It reminded her of the image on her medallion.

"Thank you," she said as she braided the feather into her hair.

A blessing, she thought. *Maybe this quest isn't hopeless after all.* She frowned. Where had that thought come from? A difficult quest, yes, traveling by herself to Swedetown. But hopeless? She hadn't thought of it that way at the beginning.

Transformation is always difficult, she reminded herself. *And this transformation is but a part of the Great Dance.*

She allowed herself a couple of skipping steps along River's sands before settling back into her walking stride.

She'd be dancing with River soon enough. Best to husband her strength.

What remained of the City still lay ahead of her.

Soon enough a low, broken dike intruded upon the sandy river shoreline. Marthe pulled on her boots, then scrambled on top of the dike, following a thin path that grew wider. The only sign of settlement was a field of stumps where someone had been cutting the cottonwood and ash groves near the dike.

That changed. The stump field gave way to the broken, scorched remains of buildings and twisted, scarred lumps of metal that had once been equipment of some sort. Marthe quickened her step, these first signs of the Old Ones making her nervous. She came to a tall, tightly woven wire fence that ran up over the top of the dike and down into River. On the other side of the fence, away from the river, a crude settlement of shacks and lean-tos huddled against the fence, some using the wire as essential framework. A gate sat square on top of the dike, held closed by a loop of wire. Marthe undid the wire.

"Who says you can pass?" A lean, lanky man clad in rags marched out of the nearest lean-to.

"Pilgrim's right!" Marthe shouted back, pointing to her cheeks and forehead.

The man went back inside his lean-to. Marthe stepped through the gate, fastening it tightly shut behind her. She didn't blame the man's challenge. Strange things lived in the Wild, human and animal both, especially if one wasn't River-kissed or Mountain-embraced.

Yells broke out below her. Marthe quickened her stride, not quite breaking into a run.

No trouble, she told herself. *No trouble.*

The yells from the settlement grew louder. Marthe broke into a jog trot.

The earth gave way under her feet. Marthe tumbled down the dike, landing in a mud puddle. She staggered back to her feet, shaking her head. *Don't remember hitting it.* She was vaguely aware of people surrounding her.

"Don't move." The man who'd first challenged her jabbed her in the chest with a sharpened, heavy stick.

"*Pilgrim's right,*" Marthe gasped. She rested one hand on her knife's hilt.

The other men laughed. "Pilgrim's right," one of them sneered. "Who goes on pilgrimage?"

"I am River-kissed," Marthe said, touching her cheeks and forehead again. "I go to Swedetown. To *Her.*"

"Bride of the River!" a younger man yelled. "Woohoo! We've got a bride of the River, boys!"

"Let's do her!"

The pack closed in on Marthe. She pulled her knife, sickeningly aware of the odds against her. Five men. Three were old and frail, possibly enough for her to best in combat, but two were younger. Scraggly-toothed and scrawny, but young. Those two advanced closer, grinning at Marthe.

"Come dance with us, baby," one crooned, leering at Marthe.

One man lunged at Marthe, grabbing at her pack and spinning her around. She stabbed at the young man, unable to get any blows in beyond quick slashes. Another man jumped on her back. Marthe shook him and her pack off. She twisted free and took off running. Better to leave the pack than risk further attack.

I come to you empty-handed, oh River. It was what she was supposed to do, but her plan to discard her belongings had been more systematic than this act of robbery.

Someone tackled Marthe, bringing her down right at the top of the dike. She struck at her attacker with her knife. He overpowered her with his greater weight, grabbing her hands and twisting her knife away. She kicked at him. He kneed her in the gut. Marthe gasped for air. His hands tore at her shirt and ripped it open, sending buttons flying.

"Aha. What's this?" he asked, picking up her medallion in grimy fingers.

No. Not that!

The man's fingers tightened greedily. The thong held firm.

"No," Marthe moaned. "Oh no." Her fingers desperately scrabbled in the dirt next to her. Her right hand found the hilt of her knife. She grabbed the knife. Thrust it deep into his gut. His eyes widened and his fingers spasmed against her throat. Marthe found the strength to shove him off of her. She pulled her knife free, rolled to her knees, and half-ran, half-fell down the side of the dike, tumbling into River. The footing dropped straight down here, bottom far below her feet as the waters closed over her head.

Marthe gasped at the shock of River's coldness. Water rushed into her mouth and nose as she struggled to rise.

Her lungs choked on the water and panic surged through her limbs. *I can't breathe!*

River-kissed she might be, but she wasn't ready for transformation yet.

I've failed. Heartsick at the possible consequences, she struggled.

Then her head broke free of the water. She floundered along the surface, coughing, struggling to find her rhythm in the water.

Harmony is broken, something keened inside her. *Harmony is broken.*

She became aware of the knife still in her hand and let River take it. She felt at her neck for the medallion. It still hung in place. Marthe relaxed. Her arms suddenly, joyously, found River's rhythm, moving in harmony with her legs. She coughed but even the cough bringing up the last dregs of water in her system was now in harmony with the rest of her body and with River.

Free.

But at what cost? No food, no other clothing, no money, nothing but what she stood in. And it was at least another full day's journey to Swedetown.

River takes and River gives. What happened from here would be in River's hands.

"Help me," she whispered to River. "Help me to Swedetown. It's not time for me to change yet."

It was too bad she couldn't swim all the way to Swedetown. After Transformation, she could.

But she wasn't transformed yet.

"Hoy! Swimmer!" The high-pitched call came from midriver.

Marthe spotted a canoe downriver, its rider paddling upriver smoothly. She hesitated, then waved a hand.

"Help?" she ventured, taking a chance. The paddler sounded female. Hopefully not another predator from the City.

"Be right there," the paddler answered.

Marthe sidestroked toward the canoe. She grabbed the bow, hugging it tight.

"You have problems with the Juniors?" the paddler asked. This close, Marthe could see she was, indeed, female.

"They attacked me. Had to leave my pack."

The woman shook her head ruefully. "Roll on in. You're River-kissed, aren't you?"

"Yes," Marthe gasped. She carefully climbed in.

"Bastards." The woman spun the canoe around. "Catch your breath. My name's Rehana, of Swedetown."

Swedetown reaches out to me already? She breathed silent thanks to River.

"Marthe," she said. "On pilgrimage. To Swedetown."

"Marthe of the Mountain's Child, right?"

"How did you know?"

Rehana laughed. "Jehan sent Butrille a message. And the Hidden Mother's waiting. I hoped it was you I'd spotted. But I wasn't sure."

Marthe felt her neck. The skin moved more easily under her fingers than it had the night before.

"I thought I had two more days to travel."

"Oh you would if you were still on land," Rehana said. "But Hidden Mother wants you. *Now*." She dug in hard with her paddle. "So off to Hidden Mother we go."

"I'll help." Marthe looked around the canoe for a second paddle.

"Sit back and rest. You'll need your strength soon enough."

Marthe sprawled against the canoe's bow, her gut

tightening into icy nervous shards. She pulled the remains of her ruined shirt across her chest to shelter her skin from the Sun and fingered the medallion. The upriver breeze ruffled her wet hair, and the forgotten eagle feather brushed across Marthe's fingers, still there despite her battle.

Marthe untangled the feather. *Blessing of the eagle.* It was miraculous that the feather had managed to remain twined in her hair.

Now she wondered if the feather was meant to relay Hidden Mother's urgency. A shiver ran through Marthe's body, and she hugged herself tightly. A creepy-crawlie feeling like maggots working under her skin tickled down her ribs.

The Change is coming, she realized, as the shivers grew stronger. Rehana lay her paddle down and crawled forward, gently pulling Marthe flat, slipping off her pants and shirt before wrapping her body in a tarp.

"Change's coming fast," Rehana said. "Hidden Mother's in a hurry. This'll keep you safe from the Sun while it happens."

"Thank you." Marthe closed her eyes gratefully, clutching the eagle feather in her hand.

THE SKIN MOVED EASILY AWAY from the gill slits in Marthe's neck by the time they reached Swedetown. She still had her feet and could breath air but her sides felt stiff and scaly. The Change was beginning. She wanted to jump into the water and finish it.

Not yet.

Butrille himself splashed out from the riverbank, grabbing the canoe's bow and peering down at Marthe on the canoe's bottom. Marthe recognized him through blurry eyes, blinking hard as she sat up. It had been years since he'd visited Jehan, but he didn't seem to have changed.

"It's her?" he asked Rehana.

"Her," Rehana said. "Juniors tried to take her. She fled to the River. She's changing even as we speak."

"You've a token for Her?" Butrille growled at Marthe.

Wordlessly, she offered the feather. Butrille looked at it and nodded. "Give that to Her." He scooped Marthe into his arms and carried her ashore.

A distant trill of musical notes echoed from the town. A woman's voice rose high and raspy, containing a liquid fullness that provoked an aching loneliness deep in Marthe's heart.

"Hear her?" Butrille asked Marthe. "She's singing for you."

Marthe strained in his arms, longing to join the music. Butrille laughed softly.

"I'll get you there, bride of the River. I'll get you to her."

He carried Marthe through the shacks and huts that made up Swedetown. She coughed as a whiff of cedar smoke swirled around them. When she was done coughing, the music rang out stronger than ever. Two guitars and a fiddle sang a haunting, sweet dance, skirling around the steady beat of hand-slapped drums. Marthe twitched in rhythm to the drumbeats that resonated deep throughout her body.

At last they stopped in front of a planked longhouse. Butrille eased Marthe down, holding her steady until she stood without swaying. He pulled the door open as the fiddle keened through an intricate reel. A wave of cedar smoke washed over Marthe as the door opened, but this time she didn't cough. Instead she picked up the beat of the drums and danced inside, turning to the right and picking up the step as she joined the dancers.

She twirled to the beat. The music and the cedar smoke twined around her like the River's currents. She weaved in and out with the masked dancers as one by one they stepped into the open space in front of the Fire to perform their solo piece of the Great Work.

Then it was her turn to dance. The slashing joy of the fiddle carried Marthe into the great open space. She danced the simple beginnings of the Mountain's Child. She danced Jehan's settlement, and the old highway, now cracked and covered with weeds and trees. She danced her walk to the Great River, danced the eagle chasing the gulls away from the salmon carcass.

She danced her attack, and Rehana's rescue. She danced the changes she felt throbbing through her body as she rode in the canoe, surging and ebbing like the tides on the river.

She danced her arrival at Swedetown, ending on the high, quavering, trembling pitch of the fiddle.

Fiddle and guitars and drums stopped on that single, sharp, hard, high note. Marthe quivered in front of the Great Fire. She held the eagle feather in the trembling fingers of her left hand. The medallion dangled from her right hand. No sound stirred through the longhouse, save for the soft crackles of the Great Fire.

Hidden Mother came forward. She bowed low to Marthe and eased first the eagle feather, then the medallion from Marthe's numb fingers. Marthe would have dropped to her knees in front of Hidden Mother, but she could no longer feel them.

"Who are you?" Hidden Mother asked.

"Bride of the River," Marthe croaked.

Hidden Mother stroked Marthe's brow with the eagle feather. "And you came from?"

"Mountain's Child," Marthe answered, her tongue growing shorter and tighter.

"And what do you seek, Mountain's Child, Bride of the River?"

"Protection for those along the Child," Marthe husked, remembering the words Jehan had taught her so many years before. "Protection, and River's gift to the Mountain."

Hidden Mother surveyed Marthe. "What price do you offer?"

"Myself," Marthe breathed, with the last of her voice. Even as she spoke, the final transformation washed over her body. She fell onto the ground in front of Hidden Mother, flapping her tail. Had she timed it right?

Hidden Mother knelt next to Marthe. She bowed low. Then she raised her hands to the sky, calling out in a high, liquid voice.

River stirred.

Hidden Mother called again. Hands touched Marthe, lifting her body, guiding her out the door and back down the path to River.

Hidden Mother called a third time.

River answered, surging gently through the village to reach Marthe's twisting, long body.

Come to me, my child, he whispered through Marthe's whole body. *The time to dance has begun.*

Marthe yearned to dance with him. But something held her back. She turned her great eye toward Hidden Mother, trying to ask through fins and twist.

Hidden Mother laughed. "Your request is granted. The people of the Mountain's Child will live in peace with

River's protection upon them, as long as they walk in harmony with River and the Child. You have done well, oh Mountain's Child. Go now to River's depths, and dance in his arms, till we meet again."

My work is done, Marthe thought. She twisted away from the hands of Swedetown and deep into River's waiting arms. One fleeting memory of the Mountain and its snows came to her with a faint taste of the Mountain's Child amongst River's waters.

Then she tasted more little rivers and creeks in River's depths, and was gone amongst River's song, her voice but a tiny thread amongst the whole.

River-kissed. River-blessed.

Bride of the River.

If you're a Pacific Northwest science fiction and fantasy writer of a certain era, all you have to do when discussing how a particular book, anthology, or whatever idea emerged is to say: "It happened at RadCon."

So true for this story. Alma Alexander grinned at me, leaned over our table in the coffeeshop, and told me about her idea for an anthology, to be called RIVER, with a river map as the table of contents. Stories were set all along this primordial river, of differing moods and types.

I immediately thought of the Columbia, between the Sandy River and Clatskanie. We had been spending time with friends in Clatskanie, and driving the tidelands. Between that—and my exposure to the rivers of Wy'East (Mt. Hood), "River-Kissed" was born, in part drafted in a lovely bookshop near the Sandy River which, alas, no longer exists.

7

AMULET, CUDGEL

omeone's coming. Startled, Anna looked up from her workbench as the magic warning drew her attention away from the amulet she was working on, worry choking her throat. Had the Queen's Justice broken through her location charm? Or was it just one of the street kids trying to break through her sparse protection spells on a dare? *Street kids,* she decided, reaching for the cudgel hidden under her table. The warning lacked the urgency the Justice would trigger, and the kids had been poking around her defenses at night. This batch had forgotten the rumors of what she had been.

Not that it mattered. Anna the jeweler and ex-prisoner had little power left of her own. What protection she had would come from this heavy club Grip made for her before—

Anna shied away from that thought, fingers tightening on the wood and iron cudgel as she pulled it from its hooks. She half-rose, club in hand, as the door opened. An older, stoop-shouldered dark-haired man entered. Anna replaced the club onto its hooks but kept her fingers on it, still wary.

He didn't move like an older man. Age fit him loosely, as if it were something assumed rather than imposed by time dragging at his soul. Even as he squinted at the cheap amulet bags she hung by the door, he failed to peer at the fertility charms like her typical older male customer did. Had one of the street kids figured out enough magic to mask themselves?

"May I help you?" she asked.

The man startled, and for a moment his visage flickered. Anna tightened her grip on the club again. He looked around the shop until he spotted her, half-hidden behind the big counters that hid her best wares. Had she imagined that flicker? Tension tightened her shoulders.

"I'm fine right now. Thank you."

"Just ask if you have any questions." Anna watched warily as he turned back to the bone and thong necklaces on the wall, moving past the fertility charms. Age wrapped him now, his hands quivering slightly as he fingered a carved antler meant to ease morning pains. She saw no more signs that he was anything other than what he appeared to be.

She sighed, releasing the cudgel with a rattle that made the man flinch. *False alarm.* It happened. Reluctantly she turned back to the cheap necklace on her bead board. The amulet that went with it was a tricky thing. Commissioned by Hopeless Avenue's boss card sharp and controller, Rikko, it was a silver wire-wrapped garnet meant to enclose a hidden spell to ensure his mistress's fidelity. Rikko being who and what he was, the garnet was flawed. Several years before—*it*—had happened, safeguarding a spell like this even with the difficulties flawed garnet presented would have been simple.

Not now. Not with a spell to be enclosed inside garnet,

one of the hardest gems to enchant. She carefully picked up the garnet. A few breaths, and she summoned the green spellfire in her left hand. When it spun in yellow-bordered green, she brought her hands together and whispered the binding spell. For a moment the blood red glow from the awakened magic within the stone shone through her fingers. Then a faint, sickish yellow-green glow dominated. The spellfire popped, lighting up the shop and stinging her hands. She juggled the garnet back and forth between her palms until it cooled enough to be put back down on the board. Then she sighed, grabbed her jeweler's glass, and studied the garnet to ensure that it could still hold a spell.

Amber flashed in front of her eyes. She looked up. The man stood on the other side of her cases. Familiar, younger, features marked his lined face.

Anna slid as far away from him as she could go as a smile twisted his lips. He extended his right hand palm up, fingers tightly clasped around the bright golden light of a wakened stone that spilled between the gaps between his digits. Anna closed her eyes to avoid seeing it.

"No. Take that stone away," she choked, keeping her eyes locked hard and shut against it. "Please. Just take it away. Yigober up the street will help you."

"I thought you would be glad to see me, Anna," he said, his voice curling deep and seductively into her guts. Anna shuddered, fighting her deepest desire to look. *Cold fire burning up and down my manacled arms* whispered through her memories, the *cold fire* masking even deeper remembered agonies from the Queen's Prison, Magician's Section Number Two.

"Go away," she whispered. "The Justice will have us both."

"Since when did Glory fear the Queen's Justice?"

"Queen's Prison, Magician's Section Number Two. I am not Glory. I never was Glory. Just Anna."

"Oh Glory, what did they do to you?" Pity worked better than seduction. Anna opened her eyes to gaze on a polished crystal of rutilated quartz, the needled inclusions glowing bright gold inside the clear stone.

She looked up at him and his face transformed from that of a world-weary, weather-beaten aged man she barely recognized to the Jarrod she remembered, his gold-flecked blue eyes clear and sharp, face unlined, hair golden instead of silver.

"Is it really you, Jarrod?" she asked, her voice cracking. Then the cold fire trickled from her wrists to her elbows and she looked away. "Don't you have better things to do than tempt a fallen magician? Or has Kira tired of you?" Kira, who had seized the power that should have gone to Anna. Kira the betrayer, now the Glorianna.

Jarrod snorted. "Once she gained power she had no more time for me." He stroked Anna's cheek with his free hand. "Glorianna." A compulsion crept into his voice. "Pick it up."

Her right hand crept forward unbidden until Anna seized it with her left and pulled it away. She tucked them under her trousered legs, hoping that would be enough.

"No."

He frowned at her. "Gods above, what did they do to my Glory?"

"Glory never existed, and the part of Anna that let her pretend to be Glory died in the Queen's Prison." She looked away from the golden needles in the clear stone that kept calling to her, trying to focus on the flawed garnet. "I'm no more than plain Anna now. Just go away. Please. If the Queen's Justice turns a scrying crystal on me now and sees that stone here, I'll lose Anna." *Like Gray—no, Grip.*

"Have you been looking at the sky? We thought the stars spoke strongly for regime change when we acted before—but they're even stronger now. It's our time to take the power. We can do it. Take up your old skills."

"*Our* time?" She startled up as the cold fire ran up and down her arms again, nearly knocking over the bead board. She'd seen the signs in the stars, and like Jarrod had said, they were strong. *Her* stars were strong. They screamed for regime change. Not all those memories had been burned away in the Queen's Prison, Magician's Section Number Two. "You *have* your power, you and Kira!"

Jarrod winced. "It's not what you think, Anna. If you won't talk to me here, where can we talk? We need to talk, with your stars rising high."

"I can't. I lose everything if the Queen's Justice takes me again."

"You're safe enough for now. Someone wards you still; weaves the protections to hide your ties to the signs," Jarrod said. "I wouldn't have recognized you had I not already known your stars. Even so, I looked long and hard before I found *this* Anna the jeweler, of all those in the City. Be wary; his shields are beginning to fail. Otherwise I still would be looking."

"He's called Grip now," she said, her voice distant. "I do what I can for him. He made my club and my wards before he got—too bad."

"May I see your club?" Jarrod set the rutilated down on her bead board. Reluctantly, Anna reached for the cudgel and handed it to him. With a whispered spell, he brought the iron worked into the wood to a bright glow which faded quickly. "I wondered how you'd managed to stay clear of my sister's manipulations and stay unnoticed." Jarrod ran his hand down the club and the magic faded from sight. "This spell is why. It allows the Justice to monitor you but hides your location. But when this fades, Anna, she'll find you. With the signs in the stars, with *your* stars, you'll have no choice but to act. At least listen to me. I can keep you safe."

"Why should I trust you again?" Bitterness sharpened her voice.

"Anna, things are not as they seem." He gestured toward the street. "You've seen how it is. Paranoia dominates everything Kira does. Haven't you heard people's complaints?"

Anna sighed. There was truth in what he said, and conditions in the City *had* gotten worse since Kira became Glorianna. "There is one place safe from scrying for short periods. The Sea Hag, in Sailor's Row. The Glorianna runs spies out of the place. But you'll have to be shadowed again—and you'll need to lend me cover."

"I can do that, at least for the day."

"Then I'll meet you there at dusk. Go. Now. Please."

He kissed her forehead. "I'll be there." The press of his lips lingered on her forehead and she felt his familiar power flow through her, momentarily quieting the cold fire. Anna sat down hard as the door closed behind Jarrod. Then she looked at the table. He had left the rutilated amulet behind.

She had to hide that stone. It was the one stone that could reawaken her old powers. If the Queen's Justice scryed her now, saw that crystal sitting on her table—she would be back to Queen's Prison, Magician's Section Number Two.

Anna carefully slid the amulet into an empty jewel bag, then into a heavier leather pouch magicked with a cloaking spell. She tucked the bag into her bodice. Between Jarrod's protections and the pouch's spell, it would be enough to keep a casual scry from alerting.

Then she turned back to the bead board, the amulet's power throbbing through her.

"Jarrod, what have you done to me?" she whispered. She could throw it away. Not meet him at the Sea Hag. But if Grip's spell was now fading—no. She needed to see Jarrod. Needed to check on Grip. What did the fading of this spell mean?

But before dealing with either man, she at least needed to finish Rikko's amulet. The last thing she needed was to have him calling down his allies amongst the thieves and petty criminals around Hopeless Avenue to come after her, too. At the least, she might earn some protection from Rikko.

Not that Rikko could protect her against the Glorianna's full fury.

By dusk, Rikko's courier had picked up the garnet and paid Anna. She secured two silvers in a bag and tucked it into her chest next to the pouch that held the rutilated. The third silver she slid into a sleeve pocket for easy retrieval. Jarrod couldn't always be counted on to pay a bar bill. She looked around the shop, throat tight. It had been a useful refuge since Queen's Prison, Magician's Section Two. Would she see it again?

She headed for the door, then stopped. She reached for a larger bag, and dropped the cudgel into it, tying the bag to her belt.

Then she left, sketching the same protective spell she

used on the door every night. It flared up brighter than ever, and she glanced around, worried that one of the few lingering on the street might have seen. But the carter down the way wearily unhitched the bony nag that pulled his rickety cart. He'd need another charm for himself and the horse in two days, if she came back. His neighbor hobbled down the street, pausing to set down water buckets and catch her breath for a moment, facing away from Anna. Another woman, the basket maker from the shop two doors down, trudged up the street with a load of willow branches strapped to her back. None seemed to have noticed that Anna's door spell was stronger than before.

All the same, she hurried away from the shop as best she could with her sore hip, scurrying for Grip's alcove and tiny shack in a crack between two buildings. Had Jarrod visited him, too?

She came around the corner onto Straight Boulevard. Grip's little nook was nothing more than a tiny wedge, enough for him to crawl back into at night and construct a small shelter. He wasn't at the opening, and she stopped, heart crawling into her throat. *Him, too?*

And then she heard a faint moan. Anna slid into the narrow passage. "Grip?"

A groan. "Gnarf snarfle," Grip mumbled, voice trailing off into a whimper.

He doesn't whimper. Anna pushed back further into the alcove, trying to avoid the slimy dirt and gunk underfoot in front of the shed. Grip usually kept it clean, sweeping and mopping after the seizures left by his own torture and imprisonment made him spew ichor. Today, the goo remained, glowing with a sickening green iridescence. Swallowing hard against the rotten egg stink rising from the trails of glop, she shoved the shack's three-plank door open. Grip shuddered on his cot, curled up, surrounded by shimmering slime that dripped slowly from his mouth.

"Grip!" She knelt beside him, heedless now of the gunk. Some days were worse than others. The Queen's Justice had been hardest on him. It had gotten progressively worse, but *this*—the blank look on his face, snot running from his nose, slobber and foam oozing out of his mouth—no, he'd never been that bad before.

Then he blinked and swallowed hard, wiping the slime from his mouth and pushed himself upright. "Glorianna," he choked.

"What? Did she do this to you?"

He shook his head, closing his eyes. When he opened them again, awareness tightened his face so that for a moment he was once again Grayton the Magnificent, the poetic charmed right hand of the Glorianna-to-be who should have escaped the Justice.

"Signs, clear," he said slowly and carefully, even as his body began to twitch. "Time. Do it. Not—for—" he swallowed, coughing as the tremors made him shake even harder. "Jarrod. For—us."

"What did Jarrod do to you?"

"Mung yet graf snarfle." He stared at her, eyes still clear and sane in spite of the shudders wracking his body. "Not. Jarrod. *Her.* Save—us." He waved a hand around them. "Speak truth—to power. Make—them—pay. Auugh!" Convulsions tightened his body and he fell over.

"Grip, you mustn't, I'll get help," she babbled. If she had to, she'd skip out on Jarrod. Maybe if she threw the stone in the bay no one would find it.

But it might find you.

The convulsions stopped. He spat. "Too late." He

coughed. "*Her* magic seeks us out. Go. Act." He began to pant, eyes widening. "All hail—the true Glorianna!" He spasmed again, gasping for breath. "Queen—of—my —heart."

Then he went limp.

Anna gulped. Her hand shook as she reached to stroke Grip—*no, Grayton,* touching his cheek, his forehead, checking his throat for a pulse even though he no longer breathed.

"Grayton. Grayton, my love," she finally whispered, anger stirring deep inside of her. The rutilated amulet warmed as her rage mounted, its power leaking into her with small dribbles, but now she didn't care. Jarrod might not have done *this* in particular, but he'd brought about Grayton's death anyway. Had he not condemned their entire coterie so that Kira could ascend to Glorianna instead of Anna, Grayton would be safe and well. The City would have swung toward justice, not power.

And for all of that both of you will pay, she vowed, tears of sorrow and rage mixed streaking her cheeks as she searched Grayton's body for any last mementos that might be desecrated by the Watch or the Justice.

Then she kissed him on the forehead and eased out of the alcove.

She did not notice that others on the street moved out of her way as she marched through the slop, and that her sore hip moved better than before.

THE MOMENTUM of her rage trickled away by the time Anna stomped through the City to the waterfront and Sailor's Row. Rather than continue down the Row toward the Sea

Hag, Anna followed the old trail to the jetty and clambered onto a low rock. There, she grounded herself and took a deep breath, rubbing her sore hip, noticeably aching now that she was sitting. She looked from side to side to ensure no one was watching, then pulled out the rutilated amulet, wincing at the tiny speck of golden light that spilled out when she briefly loosened the pouch's ties. She clutched the bag shut, glancing around to make sure she was unobserved.

Once she assured herself it was safe, she opened her hands, staring down at the tiny sliver of light still dribbling from the retightened opening. *Quiet,* she breathed to the amulet. *Still.* She blew out, damping its revealed power, down, down, but not completely out. With Grayton's death, his protections would be gone. He'd drained himself to protect her and she wasn't going to let that sacrifice go in vain, so—she needed to tap into the amulet for a little power, but not enough to attract the attention of the Queen's Justice. She eased the ties again. A softer glow radiated from the pouch. Was it enough to protect without betraying her?

What do I do if this is a trap? she asked herself. Jarrod had escaped the Justice unscathed where the others of their coterie had been punished or destroyed because of his aid to Kira. So why was he encouraging her to act now? Wasn't he still Kira's favorite? It had to be a trap.

Maybe she could flee the City instead, find passage on one of the ships serving as cook or servant. Once she was far enough away from the City that the Justice couldn't touch her, she could use her magic to serve as weather-caster aboard one of the ships.

If she could get far enough away. The amulet wouldn't like her leaving, not with its links to the City and the Glorianna. It could betray her. More than that, her deepest self quailed at the thought of leaving the City. Walk away from all those years of struggle and training, of being bonded to this place, leave it stewing in the mess Kira had made of it? She'd rather rip her heart out. No. Leaving wasn't a choice. Which meant she needed more protective magic, and damn the cost to her.

Anna pulled the cudgel free from its bag and held it close to the amulet, whispering a spell to link the two. The amulet would recharge Grayton's protective magics. She breathed the waking spell to test it. The iron charms worked into the wood glowed brighter than ever. She ran her hand down the club to dampen the spell. Together, the amulet and cudgel should protect her for the duration of the meeting. After? Well, after would need to take care of itself. If her stars were right—

She chose not to think of the alternative.

She clambered off of the rock, wincing as pain shot up through her hip and into her back, and tucked the amulet into her right sleeve pocket instead of her bodice, putting the cudgel back into its bag and stringing it from her wrist. Then she hobbled down the street toward the Sea Hag, doing her best to skulk in the shadows and keep out of sight.

Fortunately, the plain, loose-fitting brown tunic over her bodice and ragged, stained gray laborer's trousers akin to what the dockworkers wore helped her pass unnoticed through the crowd by most people. Still, Anna noted a storekeeper whose eyes lingered on her from across the street, and then further down a sailor sitting on a stoop who looked up from braiding ropes. She ducked around a fishmonger's wagon and slipped into the Sea Hag's doorway. The rutilated amulet thrummed a low, warning, vibration against her wrist.

Trap. It's a trap. Anna backed away from the door. The vibration eased momentarily, then pounded once, twice—stopped.

The fishmonger's clammy hands closed on her shoulders. "You don't want to be leaving here, lass."

Anna clutched the club in her sack. The amulet tingled. The club quivered. She breathed in, out, in. Memories of old spells flitted through her thoughts and she tensed, expecting the cold fire to start working its way up and down her arms.

Nothing.

The fishmonger shoved her forward. "Inside with you."

She went ahead in three reluctant steps. Pushed against the door. Hesitated as it opened, to reveal the tables pushed back against the wall and five officers of the Queen's Justice standing in their bright blue coats over fitted white shirts and dress white pants near a cloaked figure seated on the barstool.

They wore their best to capture me, she thought wildly, and then realized. These were the Ceremonial Guard, the elite corps of the Justice who normally were at the Palace with—that meant—

Dread tightened her throat and she grasped her cudgel tighter. She stepped inside, now seeing Jarrod standing to the right of the cloaked figure.

One of the Guard faced her. "I'll take your bag."

"No!" Anna clutched it to her chest, fingers wrapped tightly around the club, breathing more quickly.

"Let her be." The Glorianna's voice was low, soft, more Kira than imperious Glorianna. Then she flipped back her hood and laughed, her vocal tones becoming Glorianna's. "Her magic's stripped. She's no harm to me."

Anna flexed her hands on the club as the magic within it growled at the Glorianna's audacity.

Wait. Wait. She thinks I'm harmless.

"What? Nothing to say to that?" The Glorianna cocked her head to the side. "That's not the Anna I know."

Anna swallowed hard.

Humble. Think of Queen's Prison, Magician's Section Number Two.

She stared at her feet, forcing her shoulders to slump, pretending to a humility that both the amulet and cudgel protested. "M'lady, that Anna is dead," she mumbled.

"Oh? Jarrod, did you deliver my present?"

"I did indeed, m'lady," Jarrod said. "Though I will say she protested against seeing it."

Anna fought back the urging from cudgel and amulet to strike at Jarrod.

Betrayer. Murderer.

He'd killed Grayton as sure as if he had stabbed him in the heart. *Wait.* If she could lure Kira closer, between the two magics she might be able to strike.

"I am amazed you turned down your amulet." Kira stood. "I can't feel it."

Anna continued to stare at her feet. "Know better," she muttered. Dare she even think about the magic?

"Oh my dear, my dear, I know better. There is no possibility that you could walk away from your amulet. Where is it?"

Anna swallowed hard, not looking up as Kira's footsteps came closer, closer. Then one chill finger hooked under her chin, forcing her to look into Kira's eyes.

"Where is the amulet?" Kira demanded, a whisper of

the Glorianna's power trickling into Anna, foraging for the slightest whisper of Anna's magic.

"I threw it into the harbor," Anna lied, her voice harsh with the effort.

"No you didn't." More of the Glorianna's power seeped into Anna. Maybe if just a little bit more came in—the power did have its own affinity for Anna, perhaps she could twist it to her own ends once Kira had sent enough of it into Anna. But would it be enough?

Her eyes watered from the pressure of the Glorianna's seeking within her.

Hold on, hold on.

The tendrils locked in deep within her, questing. Soon the Glorianna's magic would discover the link between cudgel and amulet—

It probed deep and the Glorianna began to laugh. "I knew you were lying." Her thumb pinched down hard on Anna's chin.

Now!

Anna breathed the spells between cudgel and amulet into life. She swung the cudgel at the Glorianna, slugging her hard in the chest. Brightness flared around them and Kira staggered back, letting go of Anna's chin, eyes widening as the power of the Glorianna fell away from her.

"Jarrod!"

"STOP." Anna projected as much strength as she could into her voice. The power in it froze Jarrod in place. Clenching her hand even harder than ever on the cudgel, she raised it shoulder-high, pointing at Kira, licking her lips nervously as she hesitated. What was the mistake she'd made before? Trusting Kira and Jarrod both. She didn't have her full magic, couldn't overcome Kira if she drew the Glorianna back into her.

Kira shook her head. "Always doubting yourself, eh, Anna?" The corner of her lip twitched into a mocking smile.

"That's where you're wrong," Anna muttered, anger throttling her voice. She closed her eyes and thought about the rutilated's golden needles. Set them to dancing with tips of fire. Then she squeezed the cudgel to hurl the needles at the Glorianna.

Kira screamed, flailing at the fiery needles. "GUARDS! Stop her!"

But the Queen's Ceremonial Guard stood back, all five of them, faces impassive, just like they had done before, when Kira seized the power of the Glorianna from her nameless predecessor. More than anything else this convinced Anna that the stars had spoken.

My time, if I can seize it without Grayton next to me.

The Ceremonials would not act during a duel. They, too, had read the stars.

Jarrod tried to move.

Anna didn't dare move the cudgel from where it was pointed. She raised her other hand and snapped her fingers at Jarrod. "Stop," she repeated, her focus hard as Kira sank to the floor, hands clutching at the bronze and garnet crown now edged with fire.

Jarrod collapsed, groaning. Keeping the cudgel pointed at Kira, Anna reached down for the crown. The fire dampened at her touch and the crown detached easily from Kira's head.

Kira shrieked wordlessly as the crown left her head, twitching and writhing.

Anna looked at the captain of the Ceremonials. "Take them," she ordered.

He met her eyes steadily. "Can you tame the Glorianna for yourself?"

"Restrain them first." She fought to keep her voice steady, projected as much command as she could invoke into her voice. Grayton should be at her side right now to block any interference and watch the Ceremonials to ensure they stayed clear. Then she could meld the rutilated and the crown, make it hers easily.

But Grayton was gone. She had to do this herself.

The captain scowled. "As you wish." He gestured to Kira and Jarrod. "Restrain them but do not cuff them," he ordered.

Anna winced inside. Without the magic cuffs Kira could still strike. Kira had been careful to have Anna and Grayton cuffed before she melded her magic with the crown.

The cudgel pulsed in her hand.

Do not worry. Keep me close.

Anna's lips tightened into a thin line. She tucked the cudgel carefully into her belt, making it as secure as she could with one hand. Then she delicately extracted the amulet from her sleeve pocket.

"I knew it!" Kira squawked. "You *lied* to me!" She twitched one hand away from the two Ceremonials who restrained her, flicking her magic toward Anna.

The cudgel levitated from Anna's belt and hovered between them, blocking the flow of Kira's magic. Kira squealed as the magic backfired on her, sagging against her captors.

Now.

Anna held her breath as a fiery space opened at the top of the twisted wire of the crown, the garnets glowing bright as she brought her rutilated amulet close. She whispered the spell, thinking about how easily this morning's charm had worked once the amulet had come back to her.

The amulet slid into its home. The crown flared bright. Anna held it high in her fingers, blinking at its brightness.

"With this melding, I now pronounce myself Glorianna," she said, the words rolling from deep in her chest. Power flared in her hands, guiding them to place the crown on her head. Wire tendrils pressed tightly against her scalp, tying in firmly, painfully, burning. But along with the burning came power as the Glorianna filled her, transforming Anna.

Anna grasped the cudgel. The magic within it flowed into her, and then it was still, no longer throbbing with life. She held it to her lips and blew a charm to empower it to act for her protection and control. The iron sigils glowed with a new light, and she felt Grayton's presence.

Even after death I watch, the spell whispered to her.

She blinked to banish the sudden rush of tears. Now was not the time.

She tied the club to her belt.

"Now do you question me?" she asked the captain, who bowed low below her.

"No, my lady. What is your wish?"

"Take them to Queen's Prison, Magician's Section Number Four," she commanded.

The captain bowed even lower. "It will be done as you say, my lady. But would you wait here until we have a larger guard for you?"

"No. *This* Glorianna will not fear her people. But I will walk to the prisons with you, to review the cases of those kept there." She paused. "I also need to have a body retrieved." She told him the directions to Grip's hovel. "Have him cleaned, garbed in the formal robes of the Queen's magician, and laid in honor for all to view and mourn in the Great Hall. His last acts made me Glorianna, and I would have him honored."

The Captain bowed again. "It will be so." He gestured to the youngest Justice. "Send runners to make it so." He hesitated. "Should I also have your ascension announced from the Great Hall, my lady?"

Anna shook her head. "We will proclaim my rise as we go through the streets. After I review the prisons, then we will announce my reign."

A faint but approving smile briefly touched his lips. "The prisons have not been reviewed for three Gloriannas, my lady. Your review may take some time."

"I know. I was there. My people will understand."

He flinched.

"Let us go," she said.

The Captain barked orders and the Ceremonial Guards prodded Kira and Jarrod to their feet, locking magic-dampening cuffs on their wrists and ankles. The crown dug deep into Anna's scalp as the cudgel radiated heat. At some point the fire of the crown would overcome the power of the cudgel and consume her before leaving for the next Glorianna.

But not yet. For now, both the crown and the cudgel were hers.

And if the stars were right, they would be both be hers for a long time.

I STRUGGLED with this story for many years. It had its roots set during my jewelry-making era of the '90s in Portland (yes, that was a thing in that era and I was far from the only one). I was

fascinated by a ruby red dichroic glass pendant, trying to come up with the right combination of stone beads to make it work.

The necklace was easier than the story. Malachite ovals, burgundy-dyed freshwater pearls, and citrine rounds complemented the pendant.

But the story—ah, the story took forever to shape.

8

MEETING WITH DRAGONS

You ever wonder why it is that the old stories never show old ladies with dragons? Sit down over there. Yes, *there*. Works best for me.

Now where was I? Oh yeah. Old ladies and dragons. Hrumph. No young lady is going to know how to manage a dragon. You've not lived long enough to do that until you've had—oh, say fifty years or so of life under your belt. You've got to have that wet flush of youth drained dry before you can wrangle a dragon.

Ah-ah-ah. Put those hands back up on that board. Slow and steady, keep 'em where I can see 'em. Trigger finger gets a bit itchy and ol'Betsey here has a hair trigger. Old lady eyes don't see so good. Don't move them hands. Might could be I brush ol'Betsey and she'll go off. You don't want that.

So what are you doing here?

I told you, keep those hands up there.

You looking for the dragon hoard? Aha, gotcha. Big eyes like that give your kind away every time. Gold, gems, that sort of thing makes young men do stupid stuff.

What? Why you shaking your head? Speak louder, I'm an old lady. Don't hear so good.

Girl?

What girl?

Sit *down. Now.* Tell me about this girl.

What? You say the dragon's keeping a beautiful girl prisoner here? Where on earth did you folks down in the villages get that sort of idea? Good grief.

Oh. Someone's seen her. Huh. That's interesting. Must be pretty bad eyes, can't tell an old lady from a young one.

You've seen her yourself? Buddy, I'm the only female human around this hoard. Your eyes must be pretty dang poor.

(Explosions. Alarums. Drama.)

Oops. Told you to hold still! Told you ol' Betsey here has a touchy trigger. Don't you go bleeding all over my cabin now! Hold still, I tell you! Hey Katja, I've gotta problem here.

Keep your cotton-pickin' hands off of her, buddy! Told you I'm the only *human* female up here.

Yep, that means what you think it means. Katja, honey, gimme a kiss before you show the nice man who you are. Mmm. Yes. That's a good girl. Oh! No, not *that*, not yet. We've got to deal with *him* first. Snoopy boys.

Luscious, though, girl. I'll make you *scream* after we deal with him. Give me another good kiss. Mmm.

Oh dear. Katja, honey, he's really getting tiresome. You'd better do something before I have to shoot him again. You know too much lead doesn't agree with your gut. I think it's time.

Pretty girl, isn't she? All goldy with bronze highlights? Katja's a pretty dragon, isn't she, sweetums?

Ahem. Well, pillow talk later. Don't make too big a

mess, honey. I'll go out back and get my own dinner. You enjoy this morsel. And then we'll have our own fun.

Just don't make too big a mess of it, okay?

Darn dragons. Almost as messy as men. But the other stuff makes it all worthwhile. Now where's that chocolate? Katja, honey, maybe I will take you up on one of his fingers. Not that male part. You can have that. But a nice middle finger, like he was flipping at me? Yeah. Roast it good for me. Should be nice dipped in chocolate—want some?

I HAD *fun writing this story.*

STORIES OF RUST AND FLAME

Rust and Flame is a world I'm still wrestling with. An attempt to create supernatural entities at war with themselves and with a nebulous—other—that lacks any regard for human life, I've yet to pin down just exactly what or who these nebulous beings are.

Maybe someday I'll figure it out. Meanwhile, the book of Rust and Flame keeps getting shoved out further.

9

COMING HOME

Adrienne Taylor forced a smile on her face as she chatted her way through the crowd at the reception. She was careful not to look closely at the photographs. Things sometimes—*happened*—around her mother's pictures.

"No, I haven't heard from Ruby in months. I'm surprised she's not here. She doesn't usually miss something like this," she said to one lanky museum donor with the slim figure and gaunt face of the competitive bicyclists common to the Bend area.

"She didn't tell any of us anything," she said to the rough-skinned rancher from Blue Bucket who politely asked about Ruby's much-publicized disappearance. "Rent's paid up at her storage and nothing's gone from her house. The police don't have any clue. I've been talking to them daily for the last month."

"Yes, I have to agree, these are her best pictures yet. I'm happy the Museum is featuring them," she said to the cute young Portland couple in matching Columbia Sportswear sweaters.

She fretted her way through the polite chatter. Small talk wasn't something she did well for her own work. At one point she slipped off to the lizard exhibit, just to get away and find a touch of peace watching them bask under their sun lamps. Then, drawing a deep breath, she rejoined the dwindling crowd, still careful to keep from looking deeply into Ruby's photographs.

At least there hadn't been any mysterious disappearances tonight.

"Everything all right?" Jack, the museum—curator? what was his title, she could never remember the title of the museum event organizers, even after all these years—came up to her. Adrienne gave him one of her daughter-of-the-great-woman smiles.

"You've done a great job with it. Ruby would be proud if she were here."

Jack shrugged. "I just set it up according to her directions."

"You did it well." Adrienne glanced at her watch, relieved to see she could now leave. "Thank you ever so much in going ahead with this exhibit even though she's dropped out of sight, Jack. I know a lot of folks wouldn't have gone that far."

Not after all the weirdnesses.

Jack shrugged. "Ruby's always been there for us. It's only fair that we follow through. Just wish we had something more definitive on where she is."

"Well, I'm going by her place tomorrow, make sure everything's kept up, take some valuables back to Portland with me for safekeeping. Maybe I'll find something then."

"I hope so," Jack said. "We miss her."

"Don't we all." Adrienne checked the clock one last

time. Yes! She could leave now. "I need to go, Jack. Long day tomorrow."

"No problem. Let us know what you find out."

"I will."

A bare skiff of snow covered the blacktop as Adrienne walked along the long, curving path which led to the parking lot nestled among the lodgepole pines. Unlike most of the attendees, she wasn't staying at the exclusive resort across the way, nor at any of the others dotting the Bend and Redmond area. Her chosen motel was on the highway strip near the county fairgrounds, an anonymous chain motel amongst farm equipment businesses, strip malls, and fast-food joints. It was easier to avoid the magic that way.

Once safely back in the room she checked voice mail, hooked up the laptop and checked e-mail, checked with the front desk. Nothing. No one.

Adrienne heaved a deep sigh. She *had* hoped it wouldn't come to this.

Oh well. Tomorrow.

She ran herself a tub of hot water, poured a big glass of single malt Scotch and retired for a soak and pampering session to prepare for the next day's ordeal. She would need every bit of that pampering to face what lay ahead of her.

SHE ROSE EARLY. Breakfast was an anonymous cheap frozen microwave pseudo-Chinese thing with rice and chicken in a foul sweet sauce and instant coffee made with hot water from the bathroom. Rather than turn on the TV, she opened the curtain and studied the eastern sky while she ate. High clouds skittered across the sky, the sun periodically breaking through. Fresh snow dusted the tops of the brown desert hills. With any luck, she wouldn't have to deal with fresh snow on the passes. Yesterday's weather had suggested the weather could go either way, between snow and rain. Typical early spring day.

One of Ruby's favorite seasons.

For a moment, Adrienne considered turning back, until the weather was more predictable. It might be safer that way.

No. Nothing is safe now.

One way or another she had to find out. For herself. On her own terms.

It took several hours to reach Ruby's isolated trailer. Adrienne spent at least one hour lost on muddy gravel back roads after taking a wrong turn off of the highway. She hadn't come here often enough to make sense of the maze of unmarked roads making their way through featureless sagebrush hills. She finally stumbled across the correct county road, however, and before long the kachina-like towers of the Northwest Intertie power lines rose ahead of her. Adrienne followed the road along the power line, until she reached the lone juniper which signaled Ruby's turnoff. She stopped her Subaru and hopped out to check. No new vehicle tracks marked the gumbo and gravel jeep track.

Adrienne sighed. She had hoped for more. She scouted briefly along the road, checking the muckiness of it. It would be hell to get bogged down out here. Satisfied that the road was in decent shape and not too mucked up, she got back into the car and drove along the top of the ridge for about a half mile before the track wound down toward the lavender trailer house sheltered by a couple of cotton-woods and a ponderosa pine in the lee of the ridge.

At last Adrienne stopped next to the trailer. She studied it carefully. Everything looked in order; no equipment or outdoor furniture loosely scattered about; Ruby's old Jeep parked in the carport; all the windows in good shape. Could Ruby have wandered off somewhere and had a heart attack? A stroke? Should she have brought someone with dogs—no, the Ogden County sheriff had assured her that they had done that already. But still—there were mine shafts in this country. Ruby could have fallen down one.

Adrienne puttered around the outbuildings, checking the pumphouse and storage shed. All was in order. At last, she climbed the steps to the trailer and unlocked the door. The living room was in Ruby's usual state of disarray *("Honest, sheriff," Adrienne had told the Ogden County sheriff —what was his name? "She always keeps the place like this.")* with newspapers, magazines and books scattered about at random around the places Ruby liked to sit.

Dust covered everything that had been disturbed her last visit, and there were no indications that the dust had been disturbed since then. The kitchen was clean—Adrienne's doing. She had pulled out all but the food in cans and secured in glass, so as to not attract vermin while leaving something should Ruby return and be looking for something to eat. The refrigerator was bare except for the bottled waters and juices from Adrienne's last visit. The freezer had a few microwave dinners in it, nothing more.

Adrienne proceeded to the bedroom—nothing new there, either, then to the studio. She tensed in preparation for what she might find.

At first, it looked the same. A huge photograph of the Imnaha River Canyon lay on the framing table. The mat for it, not quite finished, was next to it, while the glass and uncut frame pieces leaned against the wall nearby.

Adrienne let out the breath she'd been holding.

Then she looked at the picture itself. She frowned.

This shot had been a wilderness picture, a simple piece with no houses or roads or any such thing included. That's what she had seen when she last was here. But she could swear she now saw a path along the curve of one hill, and something moving—She leaned closer to look, and could almost smell the spring sweetness after that afternoon thundershower, see the doe with her spotted twin fawns moving cautiously out of cover in that stringer of ponderosa pine, reach out and touch that hand reaching for her—

Adrienne jumped back.

That's new!

She bolted from the room and slammed the door behind her. She didn't stop running until she was back outside in the chill of early spring while a brief snowstorm blizzarded around her. Somehow, she managed to get into the car, her hands wrapped around the wheel, shaking with fear.

SHE ACTUALLY DROVE AS FAR as the main road back to Blue Bucket.

Then Adrienne took hold of herself. Okay. The worst-case scenario had happened. Now she had to figure out whether Ruby had gone willingly or not, and whether she now wanted to return.

And just what was that grabbing at me?

She allowed herself a brief walk alongside the muddy

road before she got back into the car. Not for the first time she wished for the comfort of a sibling, or spouse, or even a close friend to help her with this. But she had held herself alone, except for Ruby, for so long that she really didn't know what to do in order to connect with someone.

Besides, how to explain it? "My mother gets into her pictures. No, she *really* gets into her pictures. She used to take me along sometimes." Adrienne snorted. No one would believe her, not even if she dragged them along on an expedition. It would be a quick ticket into a mental hospital.

And explaining it? A talent? Gift? Black magic? All she knew was that Ruby could walk into any picture—painting or photograph—that she wanted. Adrienne could walk into Ruby's photographs, but no one else's. Whatever the mysterious talent or gift or curse was, hers was limited next to Ruby's.

Ruby had never been gone this long before, however. And she had always been careful to leave some sort of record of her passing into a picture, something to cue Adrienne that all was okay and she would be back. And there had never, ever been that hand reaching out to grab Adrienne.

Then again, there was the cancer. Ruby could have passed through and not been able to get back. Or chosen not to come back. Time passed differently in the picture worlds, depending upon what picture was chosen. She didn't think that Ruby could be forced to stay—unless it was connected somehow with that grabbing hand.

Maybe that's what's happened to the others.

Mysterious disappearances happened around Ruby's exhibitions. Ruby and Adrienne had checked them out and found nothing to suggest foul play. No clues within the pictures, no sign that anyone besides themselves had crossed the threshold into the picture world. It was one reason Ruby had given up big exhibitions—until this High Desert one, as a favor to Jack.

Adrienne sighed. She got back into the car and drove back to Ruby's. This time she avoided the back room and sorted through various things she wanted to take to Portland. She then fixed herself something to eat, and dug out the lockbox where Ruby kept her picture traveling notes. Maybe there was something in there.

And maybe not. By nightfall, Adrienne was convinced. She had no choice but to go into the picture herself. It wasn't something she wanted to do by night. First light of day was best. Yes. Rule out all possibilities.

She debated driving back to Blue Bucket to spend the night. At last, she chose to stay.

SHE SLEPT FITFULLY, gaining perhaps three hours rest. By first light, Adrienne was up and preparing for her excursion. She toyed with the thought of a weapon, and decided against it, choosing medications and extra food instead. She was ready by the time dawn lightened the world around the trailer. She cautiously entered the room, opened all the blinds, then stepped forward, picking the picture up and setting it on an easel. Then she took a deep breath, and focused on the rolling hillside. She moved close. Touched the picture, smelled the sweetness of rain-slicked grass, listened for the cries of meadowlarks. Closed her eyes. Took another few steps—and then there was grass underfoot.

She stopped and opened her eyes, looking back. She could still see the studio behind her, in a small square picture oddly out of place in this wild country. Adrienne carefully noted the place markings around her, then picked up the studio and *fixed* it into place, just like Ruby had taught her so many years ago. No one else in the picture world could see this but her and Ruby.

She found a well-worn path before her, and followed it as it dropped below the top of the ridge from the picture. The doe and fawns she'd spotted in the picture the night before sprang up in surprise, bouncing away. She could now smell the faint wisps of smoke from a campfire. It didn't surprise her to follow the trail around the ridge to find a small, primitive camp with Ruby crouching by the fire. Ruby didn't look up until Adrienne touched her shoulder.

"You fool!" Ruby snapped. "You shouldn't have done this! What the hell am I going to do now—Adie, he didn't get you too, did he? Damnit, he promised. He *promised!*"

She burst into uncharacteristic tears.

IT TOOK a while to calm Ruby. Adrienne was glad she brought provisions. Ruby was gaunt, her already thin frame emaciated and the skin drawn tight and pale over sharp bones. Careful questioning revealed she'd not eaten much for ages, and had lost all track of time.

Once fed, Ruby curled up and went to sleep. Adrienne used the time to clean up around the camp, gather more firewood and water, and prepare a better shelter. That done, she waited.

At last Ruby woke.

"You're still here," she said. "Thought you'd have the brains to go back by now—before it's too late."

"Not without you."

"Can't. Can't go back."

"Why not?"

Ruby shuddered. "*He* won't let me."

"Who are you talking about? I haven't seen anyone."

"You haven't been looking. Got any tea?"

Adrienne set a pot to boil on a flat rock in the fire ring. "Who are you talking about?"

Ruby shook her head. "Shouldn't tell you."

"I'm here and I'm not going anywhere. Who the hell are you talking about?"

Ruby sighed. "It's a long story."

"So I've got time. Tell me."

"After I have some tea."

It seemed to take forever before Ruby was finally settled in and ready to talk. But at last she propped herself up against a handy stump, leaned back, and began to speak.

"The pictures didn't just happen, you know. Oh, that's what most of 'em want to think about me, that I was a major talent who exploded out of nowhere, but like any story, there's more to it than that. I spent years and years working on trying to get the shot. Trying to capture that right shading of light on the mountains, trying to catch the play of light on cirrus clouds, get the right shapes and frames and the whole nine yards."

She paused, and hacked up a harsh cough. "No one's seen that work, not since you were born. I burned all of it after—but I'm getting ahead of my story here. Let's just say that there's a lot of snapshot photographers out there with cheap equipment who could turn out better pictures without trying than I could with my good equipment and planning. I'd *know* I got the shot, but it didn't matter if I developed it or someone else—what came out of the developing fluid wasn't what I'd done. Or thought I'd done."

Another cough, and then Ruby continued. "Your father was a tough man, Adie. When I got pregnant with you, I knew there was trouble. Big "T" trouble. His plans didn't involve children. I had to get away from him. It was hard, but I kept on dreaming about my pictures, wishing there was a way I could be a parent and still keep working on the photography."

She took a swig of water. "I ran away to Blue Bucket. Your grandparents were still alive. They didn't have much, but I could still get their help and find work. They didn't understand my thing about photography, but at least I could borrow a few dollars here and there for film and developing."

Ruby shook her head. "Blue Bucket's a funny place, as you probably know by now. Some people say it's haunted. Others say folks are just inbred. I think it's a little bit of both. Anyway, I started dating this new fellow in town while I was pregnant with you. Charlie. He wasn't much for photography himself, but he liked taking me out and watching me do pictures. Funny thing was, when I was around him, the pictures started turning out. Not quite what I wanted, but pretty damn close, closer than they'd ever been. He just wouldn't let me take a picture of him."

"You didn't," Adrienne said, dread rising inside of her.

"I did. One day, when we were out in the woods, and he was sleeping, I took his picture. Boy, was Charlie mad. Chewed me out up and down, then drove me home. Never saw him again. At least not in that world. He dropped me off, and when I turned to wave goodbye, he disappeared.

Cursed me out, told me I'd learn the folly of my ways and pay someday—and then he was gone. Car and all. No puffs of smoke, no Star Trek transport shimmering—one moment he was there, the next he wasn't. I thought I saw him and the car go a little sideways before they went, but you know, I was crying and wasn't sure of what I saw."

Ruby sighed. "Well, that was no good. I'd been hoping he'd stand in for your daddy after you were born, but now that notion had just plain gone squat. I didn't develop the pictures until I took in some rolls of your baby pictures, and I didn't even look at that roll until six months after that. And when I did...well, I thumbed through 'em until I got to the ones I took of him—and there was nothing. Nothing at all. No sign that a person was in the picture, no shadows, nothing. Picture was way damn nice, though. I ended up putting that one aside and getting it blown up for a county fair photography exhibit, figuring it was my best chance yet."

Ruby gave Adrienne a sideways look. "You know that one. It's the rock and pine shot. My first big one. Took grand champion at county and state fair, both. Right after I got it back from state fair, I was looking at it when you were down for a nap. Kept on staring at it, and thinking of him—and then I was back there. Alone, but back there. In the picture. Just like we've done all these years. Scared the pee-wadding out of me. Then *he* talked to me. Told me I could do the picture-walking, but that one day I'd take the wrong picture, and go walking, and pay the price. I guess that's what happened to me now."

"So what do we do?" Adrienne asked.

"Do? Girl, there *is* no do. Not for me, anyway. Perhaps something for you. You oughta be able to get out of here. I've tried. I can't. He grabs me back every time. I was setting up to frame this picture when he reached out and yanked me in. Told me it was time for the payback."

"Grabbed you in," Adrienne said slowly. "You mean like a big hand reached out to pull you in, instead of the usual walk-through?"

Ruby nodded. "That's why there was no note. No supplies. I was dressed warm because it was cold in the studio and I didn't want to light up the heater just yet. It'd been cranky of late and I was going to have you pick me up a new one the next time you came out. I was measuring the picture when he pulled me in."

"He tried to pull me in, too."

Ruby scowled. "He lied to me, then. He said it was just gonna be me."

"Maybe he counts me as part of you."

"Maybe."

"So what are we gonna do?"

"Damned if I know."

"That's not an acceptable answer," Adrienne said. "You need to go back. You need to finish your treatments. You can't stay here."

"Might as well die here as any other place."

"Motherrrr—"

"Damn it, Adie, I don't know, all right! Give me some time to think about it!"

"We don't dare take too long about it."

"Tell me something I don't know."

In the end, she went without telling Ruby anything. She left the pack and everything else, unsure as to whether she'd be back soon, or—or who knew? If she could leave and come back, she could bring more things for Ruby, make her comfortable. And if she couldn't—well, she couldn't. There was only one way to find out.

Her picture marker was gone when she reached the top of the ridge. Adrienne looked around, swearing softly to herself. Now *this* wasn't what she had expected. Maybe she'd gotten it wrong. She circled around, checking her markers—nope. Gone. Completely.

"Looking for this?" a voice said behind her.

Adrienne turned. A dark-haired man with leaned against a tree behind her, swinging what looked to be a small picture from the fingers of his left hand. There was a faint hint of a point to his ears and his eyes weren't almond shaped as much as they suggested the same sort of elongated points which marked his ears.

Fey, she thought.

"Wh-who are you?" she croaked.

The man grinned. "I think you know exactly who and what I am."

"Give it back, Charlie. She needs help."

Charlie laughed. "She told you, eh?" His voice hardened. "She broke the rules. She pays the price."

"You ran out on her when she needed you."

"I left her the gift. Did you ever feel deprived?"

Adrienne shook her head. "That's not the point. The point is—"

"The point is," Charlie drawled, "that you want to break the rules just like she did. Don't you think she'd die happier here than there?"

"Only if you were with her."

His face froze. "That's never gonna happen."

"Why not?"

"The rules. She broke the rules."

"So you're holding that against her?"

He shook his head. "It doesn't change a thing whether I do or don't. They're just the rules and I can't change them. Maybe if I was one of the Rust ones. But I'm not. I'm Flame."

Flame? Rust? Adrienne sighed, expelling her breath slowly, prickling crawling up and down her skin. Years ago, Ruby had told her stories about the beings of Flame and Rust. Adrienne had always thought they were fantasies—not real. She looked closer at Charlie. He looked like Ruby's description of the Flame fey.

"Okay," she said slowly. "Fine. But I'd always heard that Flame stuck to a bargain. Let me go back through so I can get some stuff to make it easier for her."

"Can't do that, either?"

"And why the hell not?"

"Because," he sighed, "there's a lot more to this than I can explain."

"Try me. Better yet, under what conditions *can* I make Ruby's life—what remains of it—better?"

He blinked. Then, softly, "You have to agree to the same terms she violated."

"Terms? You had an agreement? Ruby didn't say anything about that."

"It appears," he said slowly, "that she left a *lot* of things out when she told you. Not surprising since she was unwilling to complete her promises. You don't break a Flame promise."

"Okay." Adrienne glowered at him. "Tell me. Everything. *Now.*"

Charlie sighed. "Long version or short?"

"Keep it short."

"Your father wasn't the man Ruby was married to; she

had an affair with one of us—Flame—and you weren't supposed to be brought up there. Ruby was never supposed to keep you." He shook the picture slightly.

"Yeah. Right. I don't believe this." Unfortunately, it was starting to make sense. Ruby did stuff like that; she told stories like that to make herself look good. She didn't want to think of her mother as a liar—*but that's exactly why I moved away from her and couldn't live with her.*

"Just where do you think you are now? How many people can walk into pictures? Ruby made a deal with him —we needed a child born over there, with certain talents and skills we could only get from her kind; in return she got her talent."

"Then why did she get the talent, if she didn't hand me over?"

"She kept you. And the talent. She banished me by taking my picture. I was stupid—that was how she double-crossed your father."

"So. If I stay, what help can I get for her?"

He shook his head. "Has to be of your own free will, no duress, no compunction to take care of her. She has a price to pay."

"She's dying. That's payment enough. If you let me say goodbye to her, and provide someone to take care of her until she dies, I'll do whatever you want."

He raised his brows. "That's a dangerous promise. Can you do so without trying to escape?"

"Depends on what you want of me."

He sighed. "You'll be dead to your other world."

"There's nothing left for me but Ruby. I have no ties, no connections, no one who will really care. If I know she's cared for, then I have no desire to escape whatever it is you want."

"A brave soul, indeed."

"If I even have one."

"Oh, you do." He stroked her cheek, and chuckled. "You have a splendid and beautiful soul, all choked down and tied up because of her stupid choices. Do you want to see what it'll be like?"

She shook her head. Not yet. Not before she took care of her responsibilities. That was the Flame in her. "Let's just get some help for Ruby."

"Then it will be so."

❦

ADRIENNE STOOD OVER RUBY, curled up asleep next to the fireplace, and watched for a few minutes as Ruby breathed in and out. Adrienne sighed and turned away. Part of her wanted to shake Ruby awake and confront her one last time; another part of her acknowledged that such an action would be useless.

Ruby had made a bargain for her talent; a bargain that at the end she'd been unwilling to complete for the sake of her child. As that child, Adrienne supposed she should be grateful.

But was my life any better for it? A postponing of the inevitable?

She lacked any illusions about what the price would be that Charlie would ask. Whatever she would become, it would be nothing like she was now. She remembered enough of Ruby's tales about the beings of Flame and Rust, and the eternal warfare between the two. She could feel the Flame part of her being slowly waking, taking the pitiless assessment of Ruby's condition.

How could she think I'd never learn this?

Adrienne stirred up the fire. She sat back and waited.

At last she heard the faint rustle of footsteps in the woods. A graceful young woman entered the clearing, heavy-laden with backpack and extra bags. She nodded at Adrienne, then jerked her chin back in the direction she had come.

Adrienne rose quietly. She bent over Ruby and kissed her cheek. Ruby roused.

"Adie? It didn't work? I'm sorry...."

"It worked, Mom. Just not like I had expected. See, I brought you some help." Adrienne gestured toward the young woman who was quietly unpacking her load and setting up a tent. "Gotta go now."

"Adie—oh my God. You're Flame. You *look* Flame," Ruby gasped. "What happened? Did *he* con you?"

Adrienne shook her head. Ruby stared at her, then dropped her head. "All those years," she whispered. "All that time. And *he* got you in the end, just like he said he would."

"I'm sorry," Adrienne said. She slipped free of Ruby's grasp and stood up.

She walked away without looking back, much as she wanted one more last memory of her mother. She followed the trail around to the place where he waited.

"I'm ready," she said.

"I've always been ready for you," he said back to her. "Sister. One of us. You've been away far too long."

"Just get it over with," she growled, feeling the changes creep over her as he took her hand and they stepped into that bright new world. Even as she felt others reaching for her, crying out for joy, she knew she had come home.

But part of her wished that the frail old woman could be with her as well—and, if not with her, then someplace other than that hidden hillside, waiting for death to claim her.

Someday I'll make it right, she promised that woman, betrayer though she'd been. *Someday I'll bring you on home.*

She'd find a way. After all, wasn't she her mother's daughter?

THIS STORY WAS WRITTEN back when I would take a setting and mood, then try to force it into the shape of a story. Sometimes it worked. More often it didn't. The setting that drove this story was Central Oregon, of course, roughly south of Bend.

It wasn't until I attended a photography exhibit opening at the High Desert Museum that the pieces started coming together.

Like all Rust and Flame stories I've written so far, it's not exactly a cheery tale.

IO
WITCH TRAILS

"**N**o, honey, that's not right." I checked the paper Jerry was writing for the fourth and fifth grade Social Studies unit. The other three kids in small group were writing about Pilgrims, Thanksgiving, and Early Puritan School Days. It looked like Jerry was writing about the Salem Witch Trials. Jerry being Jerry, he'd written "witch trails."

"Uh-huh, it's right, Ms. James. I'm writing a story about the witch trails."

"Witch *trials*," I corrected.

"Uh-uh. Witch *trails*."

"Jerry, hon, there's no such thing as witch trails."

Mark nearly fell over waving his hand at me. "Ms. Johnston! Ms. Johnston! There is *so* such a thing as witch trails!"

"Oh?" I decided to play along.

"Yeah. My mom won't let me play on them."

Yesinia nodded in agreement. "There's lots of witch trails out there, Ms. Johnston."

Donnie chimed in. "You haven't heard of the witch trails, Ms. Johnston?"

I tapped Donnie's paper. "Let's get back to work. You need to give me another paragraph on the Pilgrims."

"Aw, Ms. Johnston!" He stuck his lower lip out at me.

I resisted a temptation to tousle his tangled white-blond hair, and tapped his graphic organizer. "Look, Donnie, see, here's your topic for this paragraph. What's a good sentence you could write about the Pilgrims and how they dressed?"

He sighed, and got back to work. I noticed that Yesinia and Mark had taken the cue for redirection, and were busily writing, or, at least, were pretending to contemplate their graphic organizers. Only Jerry sat firm, scowling at me.

"I'm not writing any stupid witch trial paper," he stated. "I already did mine. I'm writing about the witch trails. Mrs. Osborn said I could write a story for extra credit."

"Then why is your organizer outlining your essay on the Salem Witch Trials?"

He continued to pout. "Wanna write about the witch trails. They're calling to me."

I noticed a sudden stillness among the other three at the table.

"Jerry, do I need to talk to Mrs. Osborn? Or have you visit with Mr. Snyder?"

Jerry let out an exaggerated breath.

"*Whatever*, Ms. Johnston." He laboriously began to erase the half-paragraph he'd written.

"No need for that, Jerry." I slid another piece of paper over to him. "Here's a new piece of paper. I'll take that other." I palmed it, and pretended to drop it in the recycling before hiding it on my desk. It might just be worth taking a look at something Jerry had been so defensive about writing.

He was chewing on his pencil and staring off into nowhere when I got back. I tapped his paper again. "Witch trials, Jerry, witch trials. Look at your organizer. You start here."

He frowned at me, but clutched his pencil in a death grip and began to print, pressing the pencil lead down hard on the paper as he pouted along.

"There! I broke it," he said finally. "Can I go sharpen my pencil?"

"Yes, you may," I said, deciding to save the battle over *can* and *may* for another time. The story of special ed. Pick your battles. At this point, getting him to finish a piece of writing on time was more important.

I DIDN'T LOOK at either paper Jerry had written until my after-school prep time. I picked up the half-paragraph Jerry had written on witch trails first.

witch trails

i whent outside last nite cause the witch trails caled my nam they were gloinggreen purpel blu my granpa was their walking with man from flame they wer talking about new teacher thats you miz johnston and i got skared ran away but weird scary man from rust there too and he spoke mean watch out for witch trails they are dangrous mom says and I got spaked cause granpa isnt alive no more and i was seeing things

That must have been when I interrupted his story. I frowned at it. Glowing trails? Spanking? Talking about me?

Well, as far as a story went, it was a good beginning. I made a mental note to have Jerry sit down with a story map and expand this story. Then we'd edit it for the spelling and grammar mistakes, and have him rewrite it correctly. Maybe we could get him on track for the fifth-grade writing assessment.

I turned to his essay. He'd managed a less-than stellar five sentence paragraph on the Salem Witch trials. Clearly more work to be done. But, at the bottom, he'd scrawled the following, in big, shaky letters:

THEIR IS SO SUCH THING AS WITCH TRAILS, MIZ JOHNSTON.

I DIDN'T HAVE a chance to ask anyone about witch trails until the next morning, while laminating some checklist cards for my middle school students. Penny Kennedy was running tests for her Language Arts classes through the main copier.

"Have you ever heard of anything around here called a witch trail?" I asked while trimming up my laminated cards on the worktable.

She paused, and I noticed that same quick stillness that I'd noticed in the kids yesterday, before she answered. "No. Witch trails? That's kind of a silly thing."

"That's what I thought, too. Except that Jerry Toller was writing a story about them when he should have been writing about the Salem Witch Trials."

Again, that quick stillness before she answered. "Oh, well that's probably why, then. He just did a typo and decided it was more fun to take off on one of those stories. Those Toller boys can all be a bit silly. His older brother is sure a goofball." She started telling a story about the Toller boy in her eighth-grade class and his latest stunts. I'd heard her tell the story at lunch, so I half-tuned out, until she said something about Grandpa Toller talking to Peter.

"Huh? I thought Grandpa Toller was dead," I said.

"He is," she said. "But Peter comes in and tells me all about talking to him at least two times a week." She made a face. "Given their home life, I think it's a way for him to not think about what's going on."

I had to agree with her. The Toller home life was pretty grim. The daughter, Mary, had run away just last year, glimpsed once in Portland but never again after that. The parents didn't mourn her. I'd heard all about it in the staff room gossip.

It was generally acknowledged that the Tollers were abusive to the kids, even though we couldn't prove it and we couldn't get the Department of Human Services to take our reports seriously. I'd already received the canned DHS lecture about "families of poverty." The parents were savvy enough to not spank so hard that it left bruises, but we knew the kids were hit. And verbally abused.

No wonder Peter and Jerry and Martin escaped to an imaginary world. No wonder Mary had run away. I would have too. I just wondered why the boys hadn't disappeared as well.

"Thanks," I told Penny, and went back to my room.

Jerry wasn't in writing group that day. When I asked the other kids, they shrugged, except for Yesinia. Her eyes went wide and she ducked her head down so I couldn't see her face. I wondered what she knew—the Garcias lived next door to the Tollers, and if it hadn't been that at least part of the family were illegal immigrants, I was sure that the Garcia family would have turned the Tollers in on a regular basis. They were strict with their own kids, and I'm sure the Garcia kids knew what a belt meant, but *their* kids were clean, well-fed, and well-behaved, plus Mama and Papa showed up at *every* parent conference, the school translator in tow.

Yesinia should have been in an English Language Development program instead of Special Ed, but she'd qualified as Communication Disorder with a reading disability as well, even though I had a strong hunch the issue was really language learning confusion.

On the pretext of working one-on-one with Yesinia to conference over her Social Studies paper, I took her aside.

"Did anything—*happen*—at Jerry's house last night?"

Yesinia shook her head. I stifled a sigh and conferenced with her, discussing her spelling and grammar mistakes. She was quick to spot them on her own after we went through the first paragraph, and raced through the rest of the corrections.

As she went back to her seat at the main table, she leaned over and whispered in my ear. "Witch trails glowing *bright* last night."

"Boy, I hear there was sure a dust-up at the Tollers last night," Penny Kennedy said at lunch, as she pulled her soup out of the microwave. "This your lunch on top, Nita? How long do you want it in?"

"Two minutes," I said. "Jerry wasn't in my writing group today."

"Peter and Martin were here, but boy were they quiet," Penny said.

Nancy Osborn looked up from her salad and crossword puzzle. "Jerry wasn't here at all, Nita. And Yesinia's been moody all day. Mama Ana dropped her off instead of sending her on the bus, and Ana spent a long time talking to Maria this morning."

"Maria say anything after she got done with Ana?" Penny asked. Maria was our translator.

"She went right to Richard and they took off," said Alice James, our school secretary. "When they came back, she called someone. Richard wasn't too happy with what happened, from the expression on his face. Neither of them would say much but I gather they didn't like what they were told," she finished, and took a bite out of her sandwich.

We looked at each other. That sounded like the behavior of a mandatory reporter who had made the required child abuse call. Richard Snyder, our principal, generally didn't encourage such reports because of the attitude of the local branch of DHS, but if he'd been part of the call, along with Maria, then it was bad.

Silence hung over the room like a shroud. Then Penny Kennedy spoke up again. "Hey. I hear that Kevin Andrews made Phi Beta Kappa at the U of O."

That perked up the crowd, and the discussion changed to lively reminiscences of one of Blue Bucket's own. Jerry Toller seemed to have faded from everyone's thoughts but mine.

❁

IT WAS clear and cold when I walked to my little apartment over the Mercantile on Blue Bucket's tiny Main Street. At least the second floor promised to be warm when the cold weather hit. When Dan Andrews had rented it to me, he'd stressed the low cost of heat because of the Mercantile's heating system.

I dropped my microwave container in the sink and dumped my bag of books and papers on my table. Like many first-year teachers, I spent a couple of hours every night grading and planning. It'd be nice when I got to be like Penny Kennedy and had piles of units already developed to teach.

I looked out the tiny window at the fading day. Jerry Toller was still on my mind, as well as Yesinia's comment about the witch trails glowing. I thought about another dreary night grading papers and creating lesson plans. I was far enough along that I could take a night off. But I didn't make enough money for sufficient internet bandwidth to subscribe to a streaming TV channel, which was the only TV available here. And after what Alan had done to me in the divorce, I wasn't about to go looking for another man in my life. I wasn't ready for the needlepoint or knitting clubs, I didn't ride horses or ski, I'd read every book on my bookshelf and the library wasn't open tonight.

It was still light enough for a walk. Yeah. A walk. Out toward the Toller and Garcia houses on the edge of town. Blue Bucket was safe, almost tiresomely so, and maybe I'd find out something about this witch trail stuff. I hurried into the bedroom to change out of my school clothes and into jeans and a heavy sweater, with wool socks and hiking boots.

Then I locked up (something few people in Blue Bucket ever did) and hurried down the staircase.

It was solidly dark by the time I turned down Co-op Lane, passing by the Grain Growers Co-Op gas pumps next to the Toller and Garcia houses. My plan was to walk down Co-op Lane to where it hooked into Hatchery Road, then follow the Hatchery Road over the river and back into town. It was at least a good five-mile walk, but what else did I have to do tonight?

At least I watched a pretty sunset. Once the sun dropped behind the Bucket Mountains, darkness descended quickly. I was glad for the occasional big mercury vapor streetlights that just about every family had by their garages out here on the edges of town.

My steps slowed as I reached the Garcia house.

Like everything about the Garcias, their house and yard were neat and clean. Saul Garcia had been the foreman at the Andrews Ranches for years. There was a reason Dan Andrews made that good money of his, and Saul's dedication to details was a big chunk of it. Light showed in the living room and kitchen windows, the curtains open, and I could see the Garcia family sitting down to dinner. One Border Collie curled up on a blanket on the front porch. He watched me but didn't bark.

Everything was peaceful and in order here.

Except—something faintly glowed in a fenced-off area of the yard. A faint purple line started near a leafless bush, and ran directly to the fence that separated the Garcia property from the Toller place.

Witch trails?

The line glowed purple, then green. It was hard to see where it went in the Toller place because of the tall bushes on the Toller side of the fence. As I got past the bushes on the Toller side, the lines branched out. One ran straight past the Toller house, paralleling the Garcia property. That one was mostly green. The purple line turned green, then ran to the Toller house.

The Toller place was nothing like the Garcia property. Even in the dark I could see the garbage dumped around the yard—two rusting old car hulks, a stack of scrap wood here, a stack of scrap metal there. A handscrawled NO TRESSPASSING sign hung askew from the fencepost by the gate. Luckily, the dogs weren't out tonight—I'd heard about the viciousness of the Toller dogs.

The curtains were firmly shut throughout the Toller house, which was unusual for Blue Bucket. Most locals left curtains open. Angry shouting came from the house as I followed the road's curve around the Toller place, giving me a view of the back before the road twisted another sharp dogleg away.

The back door slammed, and a kid shot out into the night. Small enough to be Jerry. He ran for the purple line, hit it, bounced back. With a cry, he tried again, then started running until he blundered into the green line and started running hard along it. Then a white light flashed, and he was gone.

I gulped.

Witch trails, indeed.

I picked up my walking pace, trying to get away from there, thoughts racing through my head. Surely Penny Kennedy knew about this sort of thing. It couldn't be that much of a secret here in Blue Bucket. What the heck was it that I'd just seen?

I didn't see the green line before I stumbled onto it where it crossed the road. Or had it been there before? I didn't remember seeing anything—and then, suddenly, I was surrounded in green light. I couldn't move forward. I couldn't move back. I could move sideways, along the trail.

Someone chuckled. I turned to see a shadowy figure.

"Ready to play, Nita?" he asked. A tall man. Or something that looked like a man, with white-blond hair and pointy ears, and slender, elongated but crumbling features too long to be real. I knew his name without being told. Marren. He took my chin in his long, almost skeletal, fingers.

"NO!" I broke away. His laughter followed me.

"Playing hard to get, little one?"

I ran hard. Time seemed to freeze as the green lights flashed around me.

Car lights flared, and I screeched to a stop, panting hard. The driver stepped out.

"You okay, Miz Johnston?" Alberto Garcia, Saul's younger brother. I stood in the lights, trembling. He'd almost hit me—hadn't he?

I was also way past the Garcia place, several miles away.

I shook my head. "No. Yes. Maybe. I'll be okay."

"I'll take you home," he said.

We rode in silence until he stopped before the Merc.

"Miz Johnston," he said, as I reached for the door handle.

"Yes?"

"Don't you go playing on them witch trails. They're not safe."

I shivered. "I just figured that out. Thank you for the ride, and—just—gracias, Alberto."

"De nada."

I carefully shut the car door, and ran up the stairs to my safe little apartment.

I stared at the time on the clock. Midnight.

Just how long had I been on that trail?

NIGHTMARES STALKED MY SLEEP. Marren chased me down trails of flashing green lights. Tiny pieces shattered away every time he touched me. Rust. He was Rust itself, Rust as a fey being, Rust as a living thing. Rust. Stalking me along the witch trails.

Jerry screamed once when I ran past him, but he was already Rust, Rust in his words and Rust in his movements, his features developing those long, slender crumbling edges that I'd noticed but not really noted before.

I woke with a start, soaking wet with sweat, and glanced over to my alarm. 2:16. A faint green glow caught my eye.

Marren chuckled.

No. Oh no. I clutched my knees, shaking with fear as a shape slowly took form. Marren. *No.*

A soft, cautious knock sounded on my door. "Miz Johnston?" Alberto.

Thank God.

I grabbed my bathrobe and raced to the door, for once grateful that the other upstairs apartment was unoccupied.

Alberto swept past me, his face grim and set. I saw a brief flash of purple light, marked with the bright red and orange of Flame. He started shouting at Marren in a language I didn't recognize.

When I turned around, I saw not two human figures, but what seemed to be bright pillars, one greenish-white, the other purple with red and orange borders. As I watched, the purple grew taller than the greenish-white, and the greenish-white winked out, but not without a final malevolent flicker in my direction.

He was gone. I collapsed to the floor, shaking.

The purple light slowly regained Alberto's shape, and walked toward me. Alberto's hand was hot to the touch as he helped me back to my feet, strangely intimate.

"He marked you," he murmured, running his fingertips along my arms, then onto my chin, slowing, then stopping, where Marren had first taken my chin in his slender fingers. "Hm. Not enough—forgive me this intrusion." He replaced his fingers with his lips, kissing my chin in a fiery embrace which was both highly erotic and yet not so.

I shuddered when he pulled away. I wanted more. I wanted it all.

"No," he said softly. "You do not know. That's what *he* would do. Not me. Go." His hands, again burning with an intimate fire, turned me toward the bedroom. "Go. Sleep for the rest of the night. No more dreams. I will sit watch."

As ordered, I slept, dreamless save for one quick flicker of Alberto.

Alberto still sat in my living room when I got up. As I walked into my kitchen, he headed toward the door.

"Don't go," I said. "Please."

His dark brown eyes were sad when he looked at me. "You do not understand."

I took his hand. Once again that intimate flame burned within me. "Tell me over some breakfast."

"No."

"Tonight, then. I'll go looking for you on the trails if you aren't here."

He heaved a great sigh. "I did not mean to mark you for myself."

"Tonight. Please."

"Tonight," he conceded. "Late. Don't look for me. I'll come. Here's my promise." He leaned forward, and kissed me, lightly, delicately, chastely.

Except the brush of his lips on mine was anything but chaste, stirring deep, wild fires within me.

"That will keep you safe," he said.

MY DAY PASSED in a blurry haze. Jerry was gone. Yesinia turned deep sad brown eyes on me and shook her head without saying anything. I could see the faint purplish tinge around her, identical to her uncle's.

Are they human?

Yet none of the other kids from the Garcia family had that tinge. It made me wonder if I was going off my rocker.

I eventually made my way home that afternoon. It was all I could do as darkness fell to keep from bolting out the door, looking for Alberto. But he promised he would come back. I did leave my door unlocked, for once not worrying about who would come through it. A locked door hadn't stopped Marren.

Instead, I puttered around the apartment, cleaning, straightening, looking at pictures from my past. When I was done, I sank down on the couch. What did I have in this life, anyway?

Those questions made me nervous. I picked up a book I'd only read once, and began to read, finally easing into sleep.

I woke when Alberto's fingers brushed my chin.

"You stayed," he said, relief in his voice. "You waited. Thank you."

Someone else chuckled, and I startled. But it wasn't the malevolent laugh of Marren. This laugh was warm, friendly, bringing memories of the summer sun.

"Berto, she's very biddable. Such is the way of some of these more susceptible humans." The speaker was a short, plump, brown-complected man with a faint hint of the same elongated features as Marren's to his ears and brows.

"This is James," Alberto said.

James chuckled again, taking my chin in his hand.

All these not-people seem to have a thing about my chin!

"Nita Johnston," he said. "Do you have even the faintest idea what you've gotten yourself into?"

"No. No. Nothing except—Jerry Toller's gone, and no one seems to be saying anything. And—Marren."

"Marren. Yes. Marren. He would like to find you again. Rust is that way."

"Rust?"

"We are the kind of Flame and Rust. Alberto and I are of Flame, and Marren—and now Jerry—are of Rust. We're—not human, as you may have guessed. Though we are of this earth."

"Jerry?"

James shook his head sadly. "The Tollers have an —*arrangement*—with those of Rust. He is gone to your kind."

"And Yesinia?" I whispered, suddenly not able to bear the thought of another of my kids disappearing.

"The Garcias are different," Alberto said. "Yesinia is young, and of Flame. But she will grow up like a human."

James chuckled again. "The Garcias are halflings," he

said. "Some are human, some are of us. Their family is old and well-respected amongst Flame."

"Then, maybe—" *Nita Johnston, you're crazy! You don't know this man at all!*

"No." James's voice was firm, as if he knew what I was thinking. "Even if you weren't inadvertently enchanted, you can't be with Alberto here. I need Alberto to stay in Blue Bucket. Saul needs him here."

My head drooped. "Then—what?"

"Two things," James said. "I can cause you to forget all this. Alberto will watch to ensure that Marren will not try to interfere with you again. But you will always need to be careful, without remembering why."

"And the other option?"

James studied me again before speaking. "I have need of someone of your experience and abilities," he said finally. "Alberto's family speaks well of you, as do others I know here. You care about your students. It was worry about Jerry that led you to walk the trails. I admire that—and so, Nita Johnston, I need a teacher's courage to help me save others like Jerry."

"Save others like Jerry?"

"From Marren—and others like him."

"Me? How?"

"You care," James said.

"That's enough?"

"Yes. Nita Johnston. Could you leave what you are doing now?"

I thought for a moment. "I would prefer not to leave until my contract for this year is finished. But then—yes, I am available."

James nodded. "You want to honor your contract. Good. I like your sense of honor."

"So am I hired?"

He grinned at me. "Alberto will watch over you, and teach you—quietly—what you need to know. In June, he will bring you to me, and you'll start your new career."

"And my pay?"

"Oh—well, we of Flame do not pay in the same way that humans do. But—" he shrugged. "You will not lack, for food, shelter, or other needs. No lack for company. Or for excitement, if that's what you want. We take care of our own, for life. And it will be a long life with Flame, Nita Johnston. We take care of our own."

"So I am one of your own?"

"If you accept my offer."

"In June, then," I said.

"In June." He slid a ring onto my left index finger. "A token, to show those who know that you are one of Flame's own."

The stone in the ring was a rich, deep, blood red, set in gold.

"There are no special properties to this ring, save for one," James continued. "If you ever have need of help from us, call upon the ring, and you will receive aid. Keep it close to you at all times. Keep it safe."

I nodded.

"Goodbye, and may the Powers watch over you." James kissed my hand. "Thank you, Nita Johnston."

He left. Alberto bowed and followed, leaving me with my own thoughts. I looked at my ring. What on earth had I gotten myself into?

Hey, Blue Bucket was a temporary job. I didn't have anything better to do, and it didn't sound like working with James—something warm moved inside me—would be boring. I had something to look forward to.

I thought of Jerry Toller. If it hadn't been for him, and his witch trails, this wouldn't have happened. Did I regret it?

No.

Well—I regretted one thing. I regretted that I'd not understood in time to save Jerry from Marren.

Then again, perhaps that chance would come to me, now that I was with Flame. At least, I might be able to save other Jerrys out there.

That alone was worth walking the witch trails.

THIS IS one of those stories with an exact, pinpointable, origin.

It was one of those in-service days that teachers dread. We had already been subjected to this trainer for a literacy workshop that was...not the best. This writing workshop was turning out to be worse.

My colleagues and I being the rebellious sorts that we were, we demonstrated our lack of engagement by doing other things during the presentation. The final straw for me was when the presenter, mockingly, held up a paper where the student had written "witch trails" instead of "witch trials," when writing about the Salem Witch Trials.

He triumphantly proclaimed "There's no such thing as witch trails!"

The science fiction and fantasy writer perked up.

"Ah, but there could be witch trails."

And I started writing. I'd always enjoyed Zenna Henderson's People stories, so this was an attempt to write in that mode.

II

QUEEN OF THE SNOWS

link in. Awareness jolts into place about halfway down the steep slope, wind whipping icy wet snow pellets against her unprotected cheeks. No time to wonder who she is, or how she got here. She'll fall hard if she gets distracted.

Ice scrapes against her uphill ski as it grabs the hard-packed snow and brings her around. She snaps into the next turn, pushing her turns. Ignoring the ice pelting her face. Ignoring the teeth of the wind. Then an echoing, faint screech catches her ear and freezes her insides.

A *familiar* screech, one she should know well.

She digs into the ice to stop. Looks around. Wavy white snow clouds blow by in shades of white and gray.

The screech rings across the slope again. A faint, distant line of four figures on snowboards rides the edge of the wind. The keening cry rings one last time, a call picked up from rider to rider. Longing burns deep within her—*mine, they are mine*—and she pushes off to try to catch them.

Another wave of snow blocks her vision. When it blows through, she's alone again, sliding to a puzzled stop.

Blink out.

"Saasaren."

She moans and turns in her bed, trying to worm her head deeper into the pillow.

"Saasaren."

The name, whispered in that commanding voice. *Her* name, though she hasn't known it until now.

A cold metal point presses into her arm.

"Saasaren. Queen of the Snows. I have need of you."

And with that simple phrase, memory floods back. Saasaren opens her eyes in the darkness. The cloaked woman calling her sits on the edge of the bed, her image wavering, and Saasaren knows it as a sending, not an actual presence.

A poniard hangs in the air between them. Saasaren reaches for it. The poniard ducks away. She snaps her fingers impatiently. Now she remembers how temperamental it is. She is grateful to Callan for bringing it to her. Isn't she?

"Come to me," she growls at it.

The poniard slides into her palm, and she closes her fingers around the hilt. Icestar, sigil of her power. She raises the tip of the blade to her lips, gently kisses it. *Welcome back, old friend.*

She chooses not to think about why she sent Icestar away.

"My lady Callan," she says to the sending. "What do you wish of me?"

"Jamarkte has been captured."

Saasaren frowns. "I'm confused. Doesn't your marriage

make him off limits to your Rust forces? Or have things changed while I've been cloaked?"

Callan shakes her head. "Those who capture him are not of Rust and Flame."

"The Old Ones?" Fear tingles through Saasaren. While the powers of Rust and Flame are eldritch to the humans they herd, the Old Ones herd Rust and Flame. If the Old Ones were angry, that would be most desperate need on Callan's part.

"These are not the Old Ones," Callan says reluctantly. "They attack the Old Ones as well. The Old Ones are calling upon us for help, and I—well—" She parts her cloak and pulls her garments tight to show the slight bulge in her abdomen. "The Old Ones think this child may be what these new intruders seek."

Callan's powers are great, but none who bear power can use much of it while pregnant, for fear of harming the unborn. Especially if the child is a suspected sorcerer. A sorcerer in utero could lash out dangerously against its parent if frightened or provoked.

"I see," Saasaren says. She traces a pattern on Icestar's hilt as silence falls between her and Callan. The poniard throbs under her soft touch, yearning for blood. *There will be blood soon enough, dearest,* she thinks to Icestar.

"Will you help me, my lady of the Snows?" Callan finally asks, breaking the silence.

"I hear and obey, my lady of Rust," Saasaren says.

Callan spreads her hands wide. "I do not want blind obedience. I have no power to compel."

"We of the Snows are our own."

"As is the Forest. Tilent has agreed to join forces."

"Then we of the Snows can do no less than the Forest. I will assemble my Court and be with you within a day."

"It may be more of a challenge than you think to tame them again," Callan warns. "The world has turned."

"My Court and I will be with you within a day," Saasaren repeats.

"My thanks to you, Queen of the Snows. Take care. Those that should walk easily with you may not do so." She bows before fading away.

Saasaren lies in bed, Icestar across her chest, assembling what she needs to know from the mana of the world about her. She discards Callan's last warning. The Queen of Rust has always been cautious. Caution brought Callan to leadership, caution brought Callan to the unexpected union with Jamarkte and Flame. What could Callan know about the Four? Rust and Flame never have known the challenges of leading the Snows. She's confident that not only can she only win back her Court, but that she can rule them.

Didn't you think that before? the mocking voice of doubt echoes deep inside Saasaren, evoking unpleasant memories.

The world changes, Saasaren tells herself.

She hopes she's right about that. Her last ride with the Four was not pleasant. They are an unruly lot, and they hunger for power independently of her.

Fourth time's the charm, she whispers to herself. *Four for the Four.*

It's late morning by the time she drives to the ski area. Wind whips waves of snow across the parking lot as she parks. Saasaren bares her teeth to the wind as she climbs out of the car. It recognizes and bows to her, capering in respectful snowy swirls before whispering away. Saasaren pulls on her ski boots, unbags her skis, fits the helmet to her head.

The wind breathes encouragement into her ear as she strides to the edge of the first run and steps into her bindings. As her second foot clips in, a low chord sounds. Power tingles up through her knees, her hips, through her shoulders to the tips of her fingers and the strands of her hair. Saasaren raises her arms high and wide, letting the jubilant cry break free from her chest, announcing her return.

An exuberant snowboarder echoes her whoop. Saasaren ignores him, extending her awareness farther.

No response.

Yet.

This is the sort of day her Court loves for riding the wind and snow. She'll have to chase them down.

She pushes off, the thrill of the chase beginning to pulse through her veins.

Find them for me, she whispers to the wind.

A swirl of dry, powdery snow caresses her exposed cheek.

BY HER THIRD RUN, Saasaren has worked over to the west edge of the ski area. She has heard the Court but not yet seen them.

To be expected. Once won, they're loyal. But to prove herself, she'll have to outski them. Saasaren is on high alert as she rides the second highest lift on the mountain, eyes scanning the trees. As the chair approaches the end of the lift, she hears the faint cry again, far off to the side of the run beyond the ski area boundaries.

She glides away from the other skiers and riders. Pauses

on boundary's edge, listening, looking. Sees the gray shadows on the slope above her.

Go, she whispers to herself and to her skis. *The race begins.*

She ducks under the boundary rope and plunges into deep, unpacked snow, riding the fall line. Her Court drops in ahead of her, angling down the steep canyon that parallels the ski area. Saasaren follows, crouching low and hard with each kneeling turn, barely turning as she builds up speed.

She finds a short cut and beats her Court down the slope, shooting out of the trees and into their midst.

"Come to me!" she screams at them. "I am Saasaren!"

They flinch away. But one rider catches an edge and face plants into a snowbank. *Kientjen.* Good fortune to her. Kientjen's the head of the Court but loyal to her. He'll come to heel easily.

Still, he growls in defiance at her. Saasaren snaps out of her skis and unsheathes Icestar as he struggles to his feet, his gnarled and twisted face evoking the juniper that calls his spirit. She raises Icestar high.

"Kientjen!" she calls. "Submit!"

"Would have been best that you'd remained asleep, Saasaren." Kientjen growls at her, staggering sideways.

She kicks him back to his knees in deeper snow. "Swear your vow."

Kientjen bares his teeth and hisses at her. A brief doubt surges through Saasaren as she remembers Callan's warning.

No. He is mine. She rests Icestar's point on his throat.

"Swear your vow," she repeats.

"You should have remained asleep."

She presses the point harder against his pale skin. "Do I need to take your blood?"

Kientjen swallows hard. "No." He drops his head for a moment and looks back up. "I swear my loyalty to Saasaren, Queen of the Snows. I am yours to command, my lady."

One down. She steps back into her skis. This time the chord doesn't sound. She chooses not to think of it as an omen.

THEY SKI BACK to the lifts. Saasaren and Kientjen catch the lowest lift back up to the top, riding in a stiff silence until they dismount. Saasaren waits for Kientjen to reattach his free foot to the snowboard.

"Where are they running?" she asks.

"We waste breath. Follow me."

"Do not lead me wrong," she warns him, putting one hand on her waist, where Icestar hangs in hidden shadow. Doubt flares. What if Callan were right about the Four's loyalties?

Kientjen snarls wordlessly and kicks off. Saasaren shrugs off her worry and follows.

This time they ride the edge of the run, not ducking away from the ski area boundaries until they're in the trees. Kientjen dives into the thickest glade, twisting through the deep powder, heading straight down into the canyon.

Before they break out of the trees, he stops. Throws his head back and shrieks.

An answer echoes back.

Kientjen points downslope. "There. Fast, to tree's edge.

You'll face them there." He points at a higher angle. "I'll circle around above."

Saasaren eyes him cautiously, tapping Icestar's hilt. Doubt wakens again.

"Go! Before it's too late!"

He speaks as he always would. But she doesn't find that reassuring. Something in his eyes doesn't seem right, and yet—she has no more time to worry. Saasaren pushes off, gliding to a small snow-choked meadow at the edge of the trees. She doesn't see the rest of her Court yet, but she can hear the sobbing cry of a human.

Feeding? She wonders if she should intervene. Once fed, the Court will be harder to capture. She climbs toward the sobs, working along the edge of the trees until she finds them in a small meadow.

At this point they're playing with their food. The victim, a young, scruffy male, thrashes through the snow. His snowboard lies in pieces at the edge of the tree line, and the remaining three of her Court are herding him, only beginning to feed on his terror.

The fear draws Saasaren as much as it does her Court. The victim struggles through the snow toward her. Saasaren lets him hope until he reaches her.

Then she draws Icestar and grins at him.

His bleat changes to fear. She looks deep into his thoughts, identifies him as a ski area predator, a thief and bully. Hardly an innocent, certainly someone worth her Court's attention.

The other three members of her Court cluster nearby. She holds Icestar high. The victim cowers at her feet. She eyes her Court. Ranimak makes a grab toward the victim, and Saasaren points Icestar at him.

"Mine," she says.

"*Ours,*" Dondije snarls in return.

"*Mine,*" she repeats. "I thank you for your gift."

"It is no gift!" Dondije presses forward. She slashes Dondije's throat. As he falls, Ranimak leaps for Dondije's torso while Wewivek gnaws on his leg.

Saasaren lets them feed. Feeding on each other won't give them the strength of feeding on this victim.

The victim gibbers behind her. Saasaren turns and smiles down at him. Lowers Icestar's point. She ignores the pleading words, hunger rising deep from within her. This hunger is for more than blood and flesh, more than sating her stomach. She's ready to drink this one's soul.

But first, the preparation. She pulls off one white glove and yanks off the victim's tasseled cap, tossing it away. Lovingly caresses his cheek, capturing one single tear on the tip of her index finger. Brings the finger to her mouth to taste.

Experiences flood through her. Catching a ride from that middle-aged teacher, he and his pal forcing her off on a side road where they beat her up before stealing her stuff. Making off with a snowboard while a kid yells after them. Other things, dark and shadowy. Cause for dread about his ultimate fate.

No, this one's no angel. And he's a perfect treat for her return as Queen. Saasaren reaches down again. Runs her fingers through his lovely, lovely curls. Eyes his strong young body. For the moment, she's tempted to take his body. But no. Such would give him power.

Instead, he'll be just what she needs to bind the rest of her Court. She holds tight onto the victim's curls as she turns her head to check on Dondije's progress. He growls and snarls as he comes back to life, biting and tearing at Ranimak and Wewivek to recover pieces of himself. She has time to feed. The three of them have accounts to settle."

She contemplates whether she should give the victim the kiss of peace before she feeds. Considers his soul, and decides against polluting herself with it. She lays Icestar against his throat, then bends and kisses those sweet, sweet curls. Icestar strains in her hand. She lets it follow its desire, sliding into her victim's heart.

The victim thrashes on Icestar's tip, screaming in agony. At last he stills, his eyes still wide with terror as Icestar drinks his blood, still aware, still *knowing*.

She lets her lips slide down his forehead, pressing deep over each eye, before she finally sips his soul from those firm, luscious lips.

It's a mean little soul, for all that. But it gives her power. She straightens. Holds Icestar high, dripping with the victim's blood.

"This one is yours, if you renew your vows," she says to her Court.

Dondije yowls, skin drawn tight over his renewed body. He lunges toward her and stops short of Icestar's point, just enough caution remaining.

"Vows before feeding."

He quivers. She wonders if she'll have to kill him again. Wewivek and Ranimak wait. Kientjen sneers. She hadn't noticed until now that he had joined the others.

The balance of power wavers. Dondije tilts his head and works his jaws. He reaches out one hand, not toward the victim but toward her.

"*Want*," he whispers. "*You*."

"No."

"Not food. *You*." He leers at her.

Kientjen laughs a short sharp bark. "The world has changed since you last woke, Saasaren."

"Worlds do not change that much, Kientjen!"

"Oh, this world has changed, Saasaren." Kientjen steps forward. "You cannot just snap your fingers and bind us back to you, even with a sacrifice. You must give of yourself."

"And who says this?" Anger pulses through her. "I am the Queen of the Snows!"

"It is a new era."

Kientjen should not be challenging her like this. Saasaren presses Icestar against his chest. The poniard remains quiet in her hand as it touches Kientjen, though it should be straining to take him. She pulls Icestar away and it glows. Touches Kientjen and the glow fades.

"What have you done?" Saasaren whispers.

Kientjen laughs again. Unstraps an ice axe from his belt and holds it high. The glow gives it away as he straightens taller than he's ever stood before. Iceshatter. Icestar's sometime matchmate, sometime nemesis.

"*Where did you find that?*" she whispers. Eons ago she'd broken Iceshatter's shaft and thrown its head into a glacier, after he who had wielded it had betrayed her one final time.

"I sought long for this," Kientjen says. "I knew a time would come when you would call us back. I wanted to be ready."

"What do you want?" Dread washes through Saasaren's veins, chilled even to her lips despite the power of the sacrifice burning bright inside of her. Iceshatter has power over her. He whose name she no longer remembers made it so.

Saasaren raises her chin high. She will not let Kientjen and the others see her fear. Icestar vanquished Iceshatter once before. One way or another, she will find a way for it to happen again.

To her relief, Kientjen hesitates. The others press close but he waves them back. "My choice!"

Dondije presses even closer. Kientjen shoves him back. Dondije leaps for Kientjen. Kientjen catches Dondije in the chest with the tip of Iceshatter's sharp pick. Ranimak and Wewivek move warily closer, lying in wait.

"Yield!" Kientjen roars at Dondije.

Dondije howls defiance.

"Yield!" Kientjen roars again.

Dondije tries to rise. Kientjen raises Iceshatter high. Red lights play up and down the ice ax's head and shaft as he brings it down hard on Dondije's head, howling curses.

Saasaren shivers as Iceshatter glows bright red. The red glow washes over Kientjen as Dondije crumples and fades.

It's the true death this time for Dondije. More than Icestar, Iceshatter seeks souls and power. She can control what Icestar does. None of Iceshatter's wielders have been able to control it.

Bleakly, Saasaren considers her prospects. Disarming Iceshatter had taken all of her power before. She's not certain she has the strength to break it again. Still, Kientjen is newly come to power. She might possibly prevail.

But it would cost time, and weaken her for what Callan needs. There must be a better way.

The glow slowly fades. Kientjen straightens up, his twisted body straightening. When Ranimak and Wewivek press close, he raises Iceshatter to stop them.

"Swear," he rumbles in a voice deeper than she's ever heard Kientjen use. "Swear to me as your King of the Snows."

They hesitate. She sees her chance and steps forward, but Kientjen is quicker.

"Do not interfere!" he snarls at her. "I'll deal with you next!" He kicks Ranimak away from Dondije's crumpled body. "Swear, damn you! Swear, or you'll suffer his fate!"

Ranimak and Wewivek drop to their knees. Saasaren hears their voices but not the words. All is lost. They're not *her* Court any more, but Kientjen's. She's wakened to a new servitude. She drops her head, staring at Icestar. Wonders what it would feel like to give herself to Icestar again. She did it before this last sleep, when she had shattered her world so thoroughly that there was no other choice. *I cannot choose that. It weakens not just the Snows but the powers of Rust and Flame.*

"Not yet," Kientjen tells them, before they fall upon Dondije's carcass. "Swear to *her*. Just like you swore to me."

When they hesitate, he shakes Iceshatter at them.

"*Swear*! On your knees to your Queen, damn it! Swear your puny lives to her!"

Saasaren jerks her head up. Iceshatter's wielder has never acknowledged her as Queen before.

"*Swear*," Kientjen commands again, voice trembling slightly. "Crawl on your knees to her and *swear*, damn it!"

Not believing what she hears, she extends Icestar as Ranimak and Wewivek crawl through the bloodied snow to her. They swear to serve her, then kiss Icestar's blade.

I should have made Kientjen kiss the blade, she thinks. *A stronger binding.* She'd been foolish and far too trusting. She should have listened to Callan's warning.

"He is yours," Kientjen says to Ranimak and Wewivek. "Leave no trace. Of him or of the other."

The two cautiously back away from Kientjen and Saasaren before falling first upon Dondije. Once they settled on squabbling over Dondije's carcass, Kientjen turns to Saasaren.

"What do you want from me?" she asks.

"To walk by your side as your King of the Snows."

She can't find words to answer. The wind twirls idly, wrapping them in a snow-laden embrace.

Kientjen caresses her cheek. "I want to walk by your side," he repeats. "I want to be your King of the Snows."

"I," Her throat tightens and she can't say any more.

Why is Kientjen different from Iceshatter's other wielders?

"*Saasaren*," he breathes. "Share with me." He pulls off his glove and strokes her cheek with bare fingers. His fingertips tremble on her lips. His eyes plead for a response. Deep inside of her, emotion stirs, something akin to what she felt for someone long forgotten in her eras of sleeping and waking.

"Saasaren. Please. This new world requires both of us to face what Callan needs." His new face is the dark gray of juniper bark. His green-gray eyes reveal a deeper knowledge than the old Kientjen. Somehow he has become even more himself, darker and more skilled than the Kientjen she has known. *Iceshatter or something else?*

Saasaren looks at Iceshatter. It will betray both of them, not just her. Without Iceshatter's presence, she would have made Kientjen kiss the blade on his vowing.

"How do I know you can control it? Iceshatter is deceitful and destructive."

Kientjen swears softly. Sheathes Iceshatter. Steps close to her. Ignores Icestar in her hand. Puts both hands on her shoulders.

"I've put it away, Saasaren. I am its master."

"For now," she whispers.

"*I need your help,* Saasaren. I can control it for now. But I can't do it alone. Share with me."

"Why should I trust you?"

His hands cup her cheeks.

"Because I have loved you from my first awareness," he says. "I have loved you since Icestar's tip called me forth. I have watched as Iceshatter's wielders tried to destroy you as it devoured them. I knew it would be different if I were the one carrying it. And when Iceshatter came to me," he shivers, "I knew this was my moment. But oh, Saasaren, I can't do as they did."

"In time you will."

"*I will not.*" He picks up her hand holding Icestar and raises it between them. "I will not follow the path of Iceshatter's predecessors. I will be its master. I will not betray you."

"So you say now."

He kneels. "Of my own free will," he whispers. "*Of my own free will.* Iceshatter acknowledges Icestar." He touches his lips to Icestar's blade. Icestar quivers but does not seek his heart. Power goes forth from her, sealing him. He releases her hand, quivering.

She trembles with him. Carefully, without looking, Saasaren sheaths Icestar. Kientjen is the first master of Iceshatter to say he loved her. The first to offer himself to Icestar.

I will have to yield to Iceshatter. She in turn will have to kneel to Kientjen, to have Icestar acknowledge Iceshatter.

Kientjen watches her, gray-green eyes steady. She looks into his depths and sees only love and a determination to win her. No previous wielder of Iceshatter has asked for this union. None have asked for her aid in mastering it.

Saasaren bows, then kneels. "Bring forth Iceshatter," she says through the dread choking her throat.

Iceshatter strains briefly toward her as Kientjen unstraps it. He growls and it quivers, then yields.

"*Of my own free will*," she whispers, and kisses the axe. It twitches but does not seek to devour.

Kientjen sheathes Iceshatter and drops to his knees. He wraps his arms around Saasaren. She yields to his kisses. They are in their own world of ice and snow as she fiercely takes possession of his lips.

It has been a long time since Saasaren has drunk so deeply of another's heart, and never before has she let another drink of hers.

SAASAREN COMES BACK to herself in Kientjen's arms. Ranimak and Wewivek stand guard over them, Ranimak at their head, Wewivek at their feet.

Callan, she remembers, with a start. *I promised Callan.*

"We must go," Saasaren tells Kientjen. "Callan called me from my sleep. There is need."

"I know," Kientjen says. "Icestar spoke to me. The foundations of Rust and Flame tremble, and if they fall, we fall, too. We must go. Together."

She summons up a snow-laden wind and pulls on her skis. Kientjen and the others strap back into their snowboards. With a cry, she pushes off, Kientjen at her side, the others behind them. They scream with the wind as they twist through the canyons. As they ride the storm, a fierce joy fills Saasaren.

Whatever happens, this time she will not be facing her fate alone.

She hopes it will remain that way.

THIS STORY WAS WRITTEN *during one of my difficult teaching years. No details, just a stressful year teaching part-time while commuting a long distance. I negotiated a three day schedule and racked up something like sixty? sixty-five? ski days for the year. I'd show up early on a weekday morning, ski for a while, then sip a warm drink in the day lodge while scribbling writing notes.*

Bits and pieces from that ski year are in this story. Spotting the row of four snowboarders in a neighboring ski run before the mists wrapped around them. Making my way down a treacherous slope. But above all else, the sensation of speed on snow.

LOSSES

12

LOST LOVES

"Whoa," I breathed, sitting down hard in my saddle so that Sox's velocity wouldn't toss me three feet into the air as he went from a full hard gallop to a twenty-foot long sliding stop. It was his best one yet. I eased the reins and let the big red gelding walk around the arena on a long rein so he would relax and air up.

Getting into the warmup arena first thing this morning before the show to iron out any kinks Sox might have was my best strategy for winning with him at the Classic. Work the old boy hard, tune up his moves, then put him away. By mid-afternoon, when our class was scheduled, all I'd have to do was lope a few circles and Sox would be good to go without risking running him into the ground. His owner would be thrilled at any ribbon Sox picked up here and it'd be another score for my nonexistent promotional campaign. I'd lost a lot of heart for it over the past six months.

I leaned forward and rubbed Sox's neck. "Good ol' fella." He flicked an ear back at me but kept marching around the rail with that going somewhere walk he had, ignoring the other horses running down the center, loping circles, or practicing spins. Even when a young sorrel filly stampeded by us, her eyes wide as she bolted, her amateur owner desperately yanking at the snaffle bit in the filly's mouth, Sox held his ground.

Then suddenly he stopped sharp, throwing his head high and snorting.

"What the—Sox! Get up there!" I tapped him with my spurs but he ignored me, his nostrils flaring wide as his breathing went harsh and ragged. I tried to see what had rattled the old boy, but couldn't identify it at first—and then I saw her. Them. A big dark bay mare with tall white stockings on her hind legs walking away from us, led by a barefooted tall brunette wearing a sleeveless black evening gown. Even as out of place as she was, no one else seemed to notice the pair. It was almost as if they were really there, shades from last year.

What the—?

Sox nickered plaintively as horse and woman disappeared through the arena wall. I looked around to see if anyone else had noticed. No one. I urged Sox forward, and he started out slow, pausing after each step for five strides, then rushing forward in a quick walk with his head high instead of level like he usually did. We reached the space where woman and horse disappeared into the wall and Sox stopped. He nuzzled the wall twice, then repeated his mournful whicker. I urged him forward. We didn't need this kind of distraction before the show started, even if it were a mutual delusion.

I'd have thought I was crazy if it hadn't been for Sox's reaction. Even from behind there was no mistaking who that had been.

Blythe and Queenie. But they're—

I didn't want to think about that. Especially not after last year's triumph. I've tried to harden myself over the years, even be proud when one of the horses I've started makes it to the Worlds, or the Snaffle Bit, or one of the other big reining shows like the Classic. After all, when you're a small-timer in the big money horse show world like I am, you have to expect to lose horses and riders to bigger name trainers with the experience to take them to the next level.

It hurts one hell of a lot more when they get into a truck wreck on their way to leaving you for that Next Big Name.

I dismounted and led Sox from the warmup arena. I'd just as soon cool him out walking through the barn aisles. Maybe then we could both forget about that illusion we'd both seen. Sure wouldn't do us any good to keep on working. I wasn't in the mindset to focus and Sox clearly wasn't in the mood either.

Besides, I might as well clean tack and make sure we were ready to go this afternoon.

"Ya looked a little shook up out there in the practice pen this morning, Joni B," Donnie Martin stopped in front of me as I checked the latigo on Sox's saddle as it sat on my battered black saddle stand in the alleyway outside his stall. "Ol' Sox getting feisty in his senior days?"

I shrugged and dropped the stirrup back down, straightening up. "Must have been a bit of indigestion on my part. Sox is—Sox." I wasn't going to talk about how my reliable campaigner of a gelding had been sulking in the back of his stall before I brought him out, occasionally coming up to grab a bite from the hay net before going in the back corner to brood. The only other time he had acted like this was the day Blythe loaded Queenie into Martin's trailer. Two hours later, he had started screaming and kicking the walls of his stall, just before Cindy called to tell me about the wreck.

I hoped we weren't headed for a repeat performance. I'd strung Sox's cooler blanket over the bars to his stall to give him some peace and quiet.

Martin cleared his throat uneasily. "Joni B. I've gotta talk."

I circled around my saddle, turning my back to him, polishing away a nearly-invisible speck of dust. "Nothin' to talk about, is there?"

Nothing except that you killed Blythe and Queenie because you couldn't stay off the damn pills, I thought.

"I'm sorry."

"Sorry for what?" I turned to face him. "She chose you over me. I warned her but she didn't listen."

His face twisted. "I thought you knew. I got those pills from Blythe."

My fists clenched. "Liar." But my gut tightened. What if he was right? I'd thought Blythe had been drinking when she showed up to collect Queenie. Maybe she hadn't been drinking. "In any case, Queenie didn't deserve it."

Martin swallowed hard. "Yeah. You're right about that." He looked down at his feet, then back up. "That's what I remember from the wreck. Queenie screaming before the vet got there."

"What do you want from me, Martin?" For prudence's sake I went back on the other side of the saddle so I wouldn't be tempted to take a swing at him. "If it's forgiveness, that's gonna take a while. If you're going to promise not to steal another client under false pretenses, then maybe I'll listen."

"I—I need a favor. I need someone to take over my string." He looked away from me again. "I meet with the sanctions committee on Monday. It looks like at least a year's suspension."

"I see." I wondered how severe his suspension would be. Most likely he'd be banned from attending any show as owner, trainer, rider, or even spectator. Besides the drug use behind the wreck that had killed Blythe and Queenie, I'd heard—things about how Martin behaved with underage female riders. And I'd had a few questions about how his horses moved sometimes. Not saying they were doped, but—

At least Queenie hadn't been put through that experience.

"Would you do it?" He looked at me now with a shy sideways smile, giving me that patented Donnie Martin half-begging, half-cute look.

"Depends. Am I just a trainer of record or do I get complete control, including those horses in my barn?"

Martin winced. "I can't afford that."

"I won't do it any other way." I rested my hand on the saddle's cantle. "Either I get complete control with those horses in my barn and no whisper of you, or it's no go. You aren't bringing me down with you by doing this the under-handed way."

Martin shook his head. "Can't you do it for Blythe's sake?"

"Are you joking?" My voice rose and I slapped the saddle seat with both hands. "You DARE to bring Blythe into this? You DARE!"

I would have said more but Sox kicked the stall wall.

"Blythe would have wanted you to do it," he said, a sick look on his face.

"And Blythe left me for you," I hissed. "You get your behind away from my space. Now."

Sox kicked the wall again to emphasize my point.

"Blythe was a *real* woman," Martin sneered. "Not like you. I could tell you what she said about you as a trainer. As a lover."

"Get. Out. Of. My. Barn," I snarled back. "You're upsetting my horse!" My voice rose again, and out of the corner of my eye I could see Kenny Wheaton, the guy who had started me in reining horses, my mentor that I usually shared a stall row with at shows, striding down the aisle toward us. Kenny had no love for Martin.

"As if you could win with *that* thing!" Martin growled as Kenny came close and Sox kicked the wall a third time.

"You need a hand cleaning out the trash, Joni B?" Kenny asked.

"I think he's leaving this barn," I said, glaring at Martin as he backed away from us.

After he reached a safe distance Martin stopped. "You'll regret that choice, Joni B. Mark my words, you'll regret it!"

He turned and stomped away.

Kenny shook his head. "What's going on?"

I let out a deep breath. "He wanted me to take over his string as a proxy for him. I told him no, and," I paused, then went the rest of the way. "He tried to claim Blythe would have wanted me to do it."

"That SOB." Kenny frowned after Martin while I went in the stall and checked on Sox. He was pacing the stall, sweating a little on his neck. I pulled the cooler down and went into the stall, tossing it over Sox. He lowered his head for me to scratch his poll, calming as I stood next to him.

"That's not all. He blamed Blythe for the pills," I said, my voice low and choked. "Kenny. Was I not seeing things?"

Kenny hesitated. That was enough to tell me the truth. At last he spoke, his voice low and troubled.

"I'm not really sure who started it, Joni B. Whether she was into those pills before she hooked up with Donnie, or if he got her into them."

I closed my eyes, then buried my head in Sox's neck. "How long do you think she was taking them?" I asked, Sox's mane muffling my words as I fought back tears.

"Since the Worlds," Kenny said, moving to stand in the stall's doorway.

It made sense. Queenie and I had won the pro division at Worlds, but Blythe and Queenie had washed out horribly in the non-pro division. We'd had a screaming fight about it, because she'd not done one single thing I had coached her to do, jerking and yanking on Queenie instead.

This mare is too talented for you to screw up by being a heavy-handed idiot! I had screamed at Blythe.

And just who the hell owns her? Blythe yelled back. *Maybe you've coached her to the point that she won't win for anyone but you! That's what Donnie says.*

Kenny's hand fell on my shoulder. "You were right then. You're right now. That SOB." His voice trailed away and he cleared his throat. "Joni B. He's sabotaging you. Getting you and your horse riled up. You're better than this, to let him play with your head like he is."

I straightened up and exhaled a deep sigh. "I know, Kenny. I know. It's just—well—it's hard. Here."

Last year, the three of us had won the Classic. Me and Queenie in the pro division, Blythe and Queenie in the non-pro, her first year up from Amateur Owner division. Kenny and his wife Annette had taken us out for a big dinner and drinks afterward. It had been the last time the four of us had gone out together to celebrate the big win.

It was after those wins at the Classic when Donnie Martin seriously started pursuing Blythe. Shortly after that she started to lose her touch. I spent more time fixing Queenie every time Blythe rode her, rebuilding Queenie's confidence after Blythe bullied her around the arena. I wondered now if Blythe had started sneaking Donnie in to supervise some of her training rides when I wasn't around.

Three months after the Worlds, after an even more disastrous schooling show and a screaming fight between us, Blythe showed up at the barn with Martin. She wore the slinky black dress and no shoes that she favored when not at the barn. The first I knew of her presence was when she came over to the gate.

I'm firing you, Joni B, she had called across the arena in her ringing, clear voice. *Payment in full in the envelope, along with my apartment key. I've moved my things out. I'm taking Queenie now.*

I'd galloped Sox up to the gate and sent dirt flying past Blythe as he slid to a stop. She didn't flinch. Sox had taught Blythe the reining basics before she bought Queenie. She knew he'd send dirt flying but not blow through the gate.

What the hell are you doing, Blythe? I demanded. *Are you drunk or something?*

I told you last night we were done. She laughed. Then Blythe turned away and went to Queenie's stall. Before I could dismount and slip a halter on Sox to stick him in the crossties, they were gone, walking down the barn aisle. Sox nickered after Queenie, unusually upset by his barn buddy walking away from him.

My last sight of them was Queenie and Blythe walking down the driveway toward the gate. Queenie walked calmly, head low, following Blythe like the good horse she had been. Blythe staggered a couple of times, but otherwise she moved with the undulating grace that had first caught my eye.

They went through the gate and out of sight.

I had cooled Sox out and put him up. He had been fussy for a couple of hours and I hung around the barn, worrying that he was colicking.

Then he had screamed, double-barrel-kicked the wall, and the phone rang.

Joni B. This is Cindy. Blythe's sister. Her voice quavered. *There's been an accident.*

Kenny's hand tightened on my shoulder and he shook me, bringing me out of my memories.

"Joni B. Don't let him get to you. You two get out there this afternoon and *win*. Show that bastard what a worthless piece of crap he is."

I gulped and looked up at Kenny, blinking back tears. "I —I don't know. Sox is off, and we saw—oh hell, I think I saw their ghosts here."

"Win it," he repeated. "For Blythe. For Queenie. For all of us." He gave me another shake. "We all get screwed over by an owner at some point." His voice hardened. "You can do it. Sox can do it. Just get your head in the game and whip his tiny little ass. Show that yayhoo that a girl can ride better than him."

I sniffled, then gave Kenny a weak grin. "That's one hell of a pep talk, Wheaton."

He dropped his hand. "Whatever bullshit he thinks about Blythe, figure that she'd want you to kick his ass if she were still around."

"Maybe."

"Look. She would have come to her senses. Even with

the pills. Annette said Blythe told her she had doubts. Then Donnie Martin would ply her with more booze and drugs when she showed doubt."

"It's a stroke of luck that he's on his way to suspension."

"So don't let him win today. You want revenge? Here's your chance. Okay?" Kenny gently put two fingers under my chin and lifted it so that I met his eyes. "He screwed you over. He stole your love and caused her death. Don't let him go out a winner."

I swallowed hard. "I won't."

"Good girl." He dropped his hand and gave me a quick side hug and patted Sox's butt. He started out of the stall, then stopped in the doorway to face me.

"You aren't the only one who sees ghosts here," he said.

Before I could ask Kenny what he meant by that, he was gone.

I GOT Sox calmed down again, but by then it was time to saddle him. I had to wonder if Martin meant to get Sox riled and edgy.

Forget about it, I told myself, and made myself focus on walking Sox around the warmup arena. I got more nods and smiles from the other trainers than I usually did, and had to wonder if Kenny had been talking. Whatever. I'd take some friendly gestures.

I kissed Sox up to a lope and before long he was cantering rhythmically, his breath matching his stride. Hope stirred within me. When Sox started highblowing like this in warmup, it usually meant a good run. He was settling mentally and physically into his routine. We did a couple of rundowns and stops. The last stop all I had to do was sit down hard, tighten my belly, and breathe a long "whoa." Before I even finished the whoa, Sox sat down hard and deep, laying a good slide track and churning up the arena dirt with his forefeet. A light touch on the rein, and he practically flew backward. As I stopped the old boy and patted his neck, I heard clapping. I looked over to where it was coming from. A wide grin split Kenny's face, and the four oldtimer Big Names around him were clapping as well.

"Let's hope you didn't just blow out your performance where it doesn't count," I muttered to Sox. But as I walked him off on a loose rein, I felt him swagger under me. Old boy sure knew when he had done it right. We got halfway around the arena when suddenly Sox jumped sideways.

"What the hell?" I yelled, even as Martin's palomino mare skid past us, Martin's stirrup whacking mine. Sox squealed, pinned his ears and bared his teeth at the mare. "God damn you, Martin!" Oldest trick in the book. Rattle another horse by riding up hard on them. Martin had called it close. Too damn close. Was he trying to hurt his own horse as well as rattle mine?

"Get out of my way!" Martin hollered back.

"You watch where the hell you're going!"

Kenny galloped up to us, flanked by Bob and Dennis. "We saw that, Martin. Reckless behavior. Jean's gone to get the steward. No more Classic for you!"

"You son of a bitch!" Martin yanked on the palomino mare's face. "You're taking that—that—*thing's* side? I can't believe it!"

Sox tightened under me again, just like he had this morning, throwing his head high and snorting. Martin's palomino rolled her eyes and jumped twice, while Kenny and Bob's horses raised their heads and followed Sox's lead. We all looked where the horses were gazing. Chills prickled down my arms as I saw the brunette on the big dark bay mare with white hind stockings from this morning, this time in the saddle. Blythe wore the outfit she'd won the Classic in last year. But her expression was cold, hard, and downright mean, her eyes only for Martin. Gentle Queenie's ears were pinned flat against her head, and the two of them ran hard at Martin. He spun the palomino and spurred her hard, heading for the back wall.

They couldn't outrun Queenie. As Queenie and Blythe overtook Martin and the palomino, they faded away. Sox relaxed under me, blowing and then subjecting me to a full-body shake. The other horses dropped their heads, off alert. But Martin and the palomino charged at the back wall, almost as if they didn't see it.

They crashed into the wall. Kenny tossed me the reins to his stallion and vaulted off, followed by Bob and Dennis. I led all three horses to the other end of the arena, quivering and doing my best not to pass my nerves on to Sox.

"I'm sorry, boy," I breathed to him. Surely the steward would close the show for the day. Damn it, and he'd felt so great after that rundown! No guarantees existed that he would be as good tomorrow.

Another chill swept over me. I felt the brush of lips on my cheek. *Win for me. I'm sorry. I made a huge, stupid mistake. I love you.* Sox nickered, and for a moment I thought I saw Queenie brushing her nostrils against his.

And then the chills went away, and Sox swaggered a little more under me, flicking a warning ear and flashing his teeth at Kenny's young stallion when the stud boy tried to push into him.

To my surprise, classes went on, just delayed. Sox delivered one of the best runs of his career. We won the class but it was close. Kenny's stud and Bob's gelding were both tough competitors.

Miraculously, the palomino mare survived, thanks to Kenny and Bob. Martin left the show in an ambulance.

I was cooling Sox out afterward, leading him around the warmup arena with his cooler on, and talking to his owner on my cell when Kenny came to check on us. He waited until I hung up and stuck the phone in my pocket before he came over to join us.

"Feeling pretty good to pick up the Classic two years in a row, Joni B?" he asked.

"Got more to live up to," I said. "But yeah." I patted Sox's neck. "Old man still has the chops. Now maybe if it translates into more training horses, I'll be thrilled."

"Isn't that always the case?" Kenny sighed. "Well, you should be able to pick up a few horses from Martin's string. The report I heard was he broke his pelvis, and was raving like he'd lost his mind." He gave me a knowing look.

"Kenny. Did you really see—?"

"I said you weren't the only ones to see ghosts here," he said.

"But how?"

He shrugged. "Years of experience. Look, we want to take you out to dinner. Me, Annette, Bob, and Dennis. You good for that?"

"Let me get the old man tucked into his stall." I felt under the cooler. Sox was mostly dry, enough that I could brush him up and put his regular blanket on. "Give me an hour to do that and get cleaned up, okay?"

"Will do." Kenny gave me a quick hug, then headed out.

I took Sox back to our barn aisle and crosstied him, pulling off the cooler so I could brush him.

No sooner had I finished brushing and put Sox's blanket on when I felt that chill yet again, while Sox raised his head. I looked to see Blythe, barefoot and in that black evening dress, holding Queenie's lead. She blew a kiss at us, then turned Queenie around and they walked away.

They faded away before they reached the door. Sox snorted, shook himself, then nosed me for a treat. I laughed, gave him a cookie, scratched his forehead, and put him back in his stall.

For the first time since the Worlds, I didn't feel empty and hurt. I still missed Blythe, still missed Queenie, but the anger that had been simmering inside was gone. I couldn't bring them back, I would always miss them—but it was enough to know in the end, that she could still choose me.

Maybe it was all a shared delusion. All the same, I'd take it. I'd lost both my loves, the woman and the horse, and yet I'd won in the end.

I ambled down the barn aisle with a touch of Sox's swagger in my step.

"Lost Loves" was inspired by a write-about-this-picture contest. I've not competed at Joni B.'s level, but I know people who have.

And, like many other people with experience and exposure to the horse show world, I've run into types like Donnie Martin.

But I've known many more people like Kenny Wheaton. Like anything else, there's good people and bad people to be found everywhere.

I3

SLOW DANCING IN 3/4 ZOMBIE TIME

Reid dropped the plastic bag and the olive oil spray, and took a deep breath of fresh air. The sweet, oily scent from the spray lingered in his nostrils. His head spun as he stared at the cardboard and fiberboard wall, his mind capering along the ceiling as numbness oozed through his body.

Does this make things better?

No, he decided, *it didn't*. Wasn't as good as an Oxy or even a beer. The only reason possible for Jeremy to try huffing was that he couldn't find pot in these post-apocalypse days. *Damn it, if he'd only asked Maria—*

"Oh, *hell*." Kat stomped into the room. "You're not dancing with the zombies, too."

"Jus' tryin' to figure out why Jemmie did it," Reid lisped.

"*He* was being dumb. But you—you know better. That stuff killed Jemmie. You want to be a zombie, go dance with one of your own!" Kat kicked the can across the room.

"Kat, sorry. Just—"

"Just feeling sorry for yourself," she growled.

"Why not?" he snapped as coherence tiptoed back into

his brain. "What the hell do we have to live for? Jemmie dead, we're living behind barbed wire and brick walls in a crappy cardboard shack, power due to crash any day, needing an armed guard to pry crops out of the ground and even then the zombies might get through—what kind of life is this?"

"It's still a life," Kat hissed. "Get off your butt and *do something*. I have enough to do to keep Lindsey alive. I'm not waiting on you!"

Reid threw up his hands. "All right, all right. It's just—don't you question whether it's worth it to keep on fighting?"

"Every day. Every damned day," Kat said. "And then I suck it up and try to make things better. As should you."

"Okay, okay," Reid said. "I'll try."

Kat scowled. "Not just try. *Do.*"

"I will."

"And no more of this crap." She pointed at the can. "Let's save what we have for something *useful*. Like cooking."

"Yes, dear," Reid sighed.

Kat tilted her head, studying him carefully. "Damn it, Reid—"

"No more. I'll try."

"You'll do your share on the work committee?"

"If it's not too late to get an assignment for the day."

"I'll pull together a lunch for you," Kat said. She strode off toward the kitchen. Reid heard Lindsey's clear, high voice greeting her.

Get moving, he told himself.

Even though it was the last thing he wanted to do.

For Lind, he told himself. *Do it for Lindsey.*

HE DIDN'T GET to the work committee in time to pull an easy assignment, and ended up doing cement hauling duty on a canal reclamation job.

Reid pushed his flimsy wheelbarrow next to the hand-cranked cement mixer. Mike filled the wheelbarrow while Reid steadied it. By being late, he not only had gotten a tough assignment, he ended up with a junky wheelbarrow.

"Going all right?" Mike asked, as Reid balanced the wheelbarrow.

"Right enough," Reid said. He guided his load over to Maria, and poured it into the form she pointed out. She scraped out the last remnants of cement from his wheelbarrow before smoothing out his dump.

He fell into the steady rhythm of load, balance, push, dump, sweat trickling down his brow and torso as he worked, not pausing even when he started coughing. *Aftereffect of the huffing,* he thought. *Smoking would have been better for my lungs.*

His wheelbarrow was full when the warning whistles blew. Reid jerked and almost spilled the precious slurry.

"You've got time!" Maria screamed. "Hurry and dump! Don't waste it!"

Reid glanced around quickly. The first line of zombies was at the trees—quarter mile off, he'd have time to dump and run. He broke into an awkward gallop, trying to keep from spilling as he raced toward Maria.

He clumsily tipped the wheelbarrow into the proper form. Maria managed to scrape and spread the cement, even as the whistles grew in urgency. Reid shoved the wheelbarrow away.

"Come *on*, Maria!" He grabbed at her and she jerked back to her work.

"Just one more—"

"*Now!*" He yanked at her tunic and they took off running. The sweet, cloying rotten stench of zombies blew in their direction and Reid gagged, stumbling. He fell.

That's it, he thought, fumbling at his belt. Nothing. He'd left his knife at home.

Then Maria grabbed Reid by the collar and pulled him to his feet, shoving him along in front of her.

Somehow they managed to make it to the defensive wall before the zombies. Reid slumped inside the gate, not joining the others in their screams and catcalls at the zombies.

Mike dropped beside him. "Damn zombies are ripping out the forms," he told Reid, handing him a jug of water.

"Cement'll be set in the mixer by the time we get back out there," Reid said, drinking long, letting some of the water spill past his mouth and down his face to cool it before handing the jug back to Mike.

"Better to chip it out and remix than let those damned zombies take it."

"Why try?" Reid asked.

Mike shook his head slowly. "Man, what's gotten into you?"

"Winter's coming. What's going to happen?"

"Something will," Mike said confidently. "You've got to have hope in the process."

"Yeah," Reid said dourly. "You do that. Right now—I can't go there."

He rolled to his hands and knees, pausing for a moment before standing. The one good thing about this attack was that he was done for the day. The colony hadn't gotten so desperate that they would force attacked workers back onto a job the same day. It wasn't safe to go back until the witches had done their scans and issued the all clear. That scanning and clearing process would take several hours—and by then it would be too late to start again.

HE GOT a bonus chit for surviving the zombie attack. Reid deposited the regular work chit into their account, but cashed out the bonus chit. It was enough for what he wanted. He wandered through the colony's narrow alleys until he reached the bar.

"Whatcha got for this?" he asked the bartender as he dropped his tokens on the counter.

Without saying anything, the bartender slammed a six-pack of cheap beer on the bar and picked up Reid's tokens. Reid examined the cans. At least they didn't look too bad, and the cans were cold. He took his six-pack off to a corner table and cracked the first one. It poured like water down his throat, with a faint bitter trace.

He was halfway through his second one when Maria walked in.

"Over here!" He waved.

Maria nodded. She got a matching six-pack and dropped in the chair across from Reid, chugging her first one down in one quick gulp. In fatigue, her features were closer than ever to Kat's—and Lindsey's.

How can two sisters be so like—and so unlike? he wondered.

"Damn zombies got the mixer," she sighed. "Almost enough to make me walk out the door and not come back. Zombies or not."

"You want to go zombie?" Reid asked.

Maria shook her head. "No. I want to take a bunch of them out, then kill myself before they get me. Zombie dancing at its finest."

Reid chuckled, and toasted his sister-in-law with the dregs of his second can. "Best of luck to you, then."

"I'm not planning to go dancing just yet," she said, frowning as she popped her second can. "But it's tempting —one less mouth to feed this winter."

"Yeah. Winter. Makes me worry. Makes me wonder why we're struggling."

"Because we're crazy-assed humans who think hope really exists."

"Speak for yourself," Reid said. He popped his next can. "My hope ran out long ago."

Maria snorted. "What keeps you from marching out there to dance with the zombies?"

"Lindsey," Reid sighed.

"Lindsey. Okay. Kids are a good reason."

"If Jemmie were still alive—" Reid shook his head and chugged half of his third beer. The buzz was finally starting to kick in with a pleasant numbness.

Damn it, I wish Jemmie had gotten his hands on some beer instead.

But Jemmie had been a good kid. A kid who, pre-apocalypse, had listened to the lectures about the dangers of drugs and alcohol. Somehow he'd missed the dangers of huffing.

Or had Jemmie gotten what he really wanted? His version of zombie dancing?

Reid finished off the third beer.

"Reid!" Maria snapped. "Did you hear me?"

"Sorry," Reid said. "Just—"

"Yeah. Jemmie." Maria gently squeezed his hand, then released it. "How're Lindsey and Kat holding up?"

"Neither of them talk about Jemmie," Reid said. "Otherwise, Lindsey's doing okay. And Kat—" He couldn't say any more.

"It's hard losing a kid the way you lost Jemmie. But it's been six months."

"Me—some days it's like it just happened. Her—Kat's not ready to give up," Reid said.

Maria scowled. "Lindsey's not enough for you?"

"Some days, no. Jemmie was always closer to me, Lindsey to Kat. Plus Kat's always been a sucker for hope."

"You're lucky," Maria said, her mouth twisting as she gulped down her third beer.

"Maybe. How do you keep going?" Reid asked.

"Day by day," Maria said. "Day by day. Some days I want to go zombie dancing. Then I think about you guys. About Lindsey. Some days that's enough. Others—no. No guarantees that tomorrow won't be that dancing day. But probably not." She rose, swinging her remaining beers by the plastic linking them. "And now, I'm going home. To bed. Tomorrow will come soon enough. I'll see you out there?"

"Maybe," Reid said. "Unless I pull another assignment."

Maria snorted. "You didn't hear the latest, did you? Priority's going to that canal."

"Then I guess I'll see you tomorrow," Reid said.

Maria saluted him with her beers. She pulled her fourth free, and started drinking even as she wandered out of the bar. Reid debated following her, to make sure she got home safely. That would be what a good brother-in-law would do, wouldn't it?

Then he decided against it. His sister-in-law could take

care of herself—and she'd be angry with him for assuming she couldn't manage.

LINDSEY WAS CURLED over a book propped up on the tiny table in their kitchen space while she occasionally stirred something simmering in a small pot on the backpack stove next to her. Reid tousled her hair and she grinned up at him.

"Mom got an extra allocation," she told him. "Crew brought in a deer. She's getting her haunch butchered now."

"She say why they gave her so much?"

Lindsey shrugged and turned back to her book. Reid swallowed hard as he noted how bony her arms and hands were. Kat could have gotten that extra allocation because of his attack—or there could be something going on with Lindsey. He hoped that it was just a side-effect of his nearly getting caught by the zombies, and not something wrong with Lindsey. A whole deer haunch was a lot for their credit status.

He tucked the remaining beers in the tiny fridge and slipped behind the curtain to the small space he and Kat shared. If he was going back out on canal duty tomorrow it didn't make sense to do much cleanup, but he could at least switch to something less stinky for Lindsey and Kat's sake. He stepped out behind their shack to check the calibration on their shack's battery.

Low. Sighing, he climbed on the bike and began to pump, wishing he'd brought a beer to drink while he rode. It took a bit of effort at first, but finally he got into the rhythm. Luckily, this wasn't one of the days he wanted to think. He could close his eyes, prop himself up on the handlebars, and drowse a little.

He wasn't sure how long he'd been pumping when the scratch of the screen door opening startled him awake. Kat came over to him.

"Lind says we got a haunch of deer," he said.

"I've been promoted to witch duty," Kat told him. Her hand closed on his. "Perks of the job—and what I had to do today. I had to clean up after the canal attack." She swallowed hard. "You made it—but some folks on the other side didn't."

His pumping slowed. "Kat. No. *No.*"

She nodded solemnly. "I heard you almost didn't make it."

"You can thank Maria for getting me out of there."

"I have."

"Kat. Not witch duty. Not with Lind."

She bit her lip and turned away from him. "With Lind being sick, we need every credit we can get for meat."

"What about Lind being sick?" His voice sharpened.

Kat swallowed hard. "The creeping disease," she whispered.

"No. No. Not you for the witches, then. Kat, she needs you more than ever. You're the one with hope—" He shivered. The creeping disease was the preliminary to the zombie sickness. If they had caught it early enough— "When did they—did they catch it in time?" His throat choked shut and he couldn't say any more. No. Not both kids.

Kat swallowed. "They've been watching her for some time, since Jemmie—" her voice broke and she brushed her eyes with the back of her left wrist, "and they did the tests yesterday. Hit me with that first—and then with the witch duty promotion."

"God, Kat—*is she going to be all right?*"

Kat nodded. "They caught it in time. But treatment—treatment is costly. Three days to three weeks—no way to know until they see how she reacts. Witch duty is the best way to pay for it." Kat gulped. "Reid, they dragged me into the office. I thought for sure they were going to accuse me of abuse or something like that—" Her voice trailed off again and she looked down. "And then it was Lind's sick, it's the creeping disease, and do witch duty or see her fade—until we have to kick her out to join the zombies—Reid, I couldn't do that."

"No. No. Neither of us can. God, Kat." He slid off the bike and pulled her into his arms. She buried her head in his chest, sobbing softly.

"Does Lind know?" he asked finally.

Kat's sobs eased. She shook her head against his chest.

"How far along is it?"

"Ju-just the beginning." Kat looked up at him. "If she gets fed right, gets enough sleep, gets the treatment at daycare every morning, she'll have a chance to survive."

"They should have talked to me about it, too."

"They said they've been watching me as a potential witch prospect for a while. Oh God, Reid—" Kat snuffled and wiped her nose with her sleeve. "And then when I heard about the attack, and they told me you'd been part of that team—oh god, Reid."

"I should have been part of the talk."

She shook her head. "It's the hope thing. I have it. You don't."

A chill made him shiver. "Why is it their business whether I have hope or not?"

Kat's eyes were dead and hopeless as she looked at him.

"Without hope, Reid, you call the zombies to you. That was the first thing they taught me today—" She buried her head in his chest again.

He didn't know what to say to that.

"I'LL TAKE Lind to daycare today," he told Kat the next morning. *I want to be there for her treatments. I wasn't there for Jemmie—I can be there for Lind.*

"If you could do that, and be there for her treatment, it'd make my life easier. I have to go to the witches early today."

"I'll be there for her treatment," he promised.

Kat shuddered. "Thanks, Reid. I—I can't—just—can't."

"That's okay," he said. "I'll do it."

"Thank you." Kat kissed him and got up. "I'll pick her up. I can do that."

"That would be good."

Rousing Lindsey took more work than usual. She grumbled as Reid pushed her through the morning routine.

"Why isn't Mom here?"

"She's got a new job," Reid explained. "She has to report earlier than I do."

"Don't like that." Lindsey sulked, but by the time she'd gulped down the small venison steak he cooked up for her, she was cheerful again.

Lindsey skipped as Reid walked her to daycare. As he expected, once they arrived, they were intercepted and guided to a side room.

"What's happening?" Lindsey asked, her hand tightening hard on Reid's.

"You've got—you've got a medical problem."

Lindsey's eyes went big. "Is it the creeping sickness?" she asked in a high, creaking voice.

Reid nodded.

Lindsey gulped, her hand tightening even harder on Reid's as a tear started to trickle out of one eye. "Am I going to join the zombies?"

"Not if I can help it," Reid said. "But that's why we have to do this. It'll help you get better. I'll be here with you."

"Will it hurt?"

"Honey, I don't know—yet."

The treatment turned out to be an infusion. Lindsey hid her face against his chest while they put the catheter in the back of her left hand, her right hand clamping down hard on his wrist. She burst into tears as the infusion started.

"It burns! Daddy, it—it burns!"

Reid held her as tight as possible, murmuring softly, rocking Lindsey with his eyes fixed on the purple solution in the infusion bag.

It seemed to take forever for the infusion to finish, though by the clock it was only five minutes. Reid held Lindsey until she stopped crying. She was shaky when she first joined the other children, and Reid stayed to watch her, not caring if it meant he'd be late for work.

"Is it always going to be like this?" he asked the medtech, who'd joined him.

The tech made a face. "I won't fool you. It gets worse."

"But it's worth it, right?"

"If it takes." The tech abruptly turned away from Reid.

Reid paused for a few precious moments more, watching as Lindsey's shaky movements steadied.

Then he hurried off to work.

No zombies intruded that day. He was whipped tired by the time he got home. Lindsey curled on her pallet, listlessly holding her closed book. Reid eased the book out of her hand and stroked her forehead, trying not to startle at the heat radiating from her.

"You feeling okay, Lind?" he asked.

She whimpered and crawled close to him. He sat with her, unable to do anything else until she finally slipped into sleep.

Where's Kat?

The creaking of the power bike told him. He went out, acutely aware of the mirror image from the previous night.

"What's up with Lind?" he asked.

Kat's lips drew tight. "She's having a reaction."

Ice splintered through Reid. "Does that mean—"

Kat shook her head. "No, it's good. Means she'll probably recover more quickly and need less treatment. But until then—" She sat down hard and slipped her feet off the pedals, dropping her forehead to the handlebars, shaking her head. "I can't do this, Reid. I can't be a witch. Not with worrying about Lind."

"Then don't be a witch," he said. "Tell them you have to be with Lind."

"They won't let us!" Kat cried. "If I were a single parent, that'd be different—"

Reid stiffened and pulled his hand back. "I could leave."

"No, no, I didn't mean it that way." Kat snatched at his hand. "It wouldn't matter, anyway. You'd still be here to split up responsibilities. It'd be different if one of us were gone—dancing with the zombies or something like that— if I got caught—" Her voice trailed off.

"You can't think like that," Reid breathed. "Are you crazy? You told me yourself that without hope the zombies—"

"I know," she gulped.

"Call in sick tomorrow," he said.

"I—I shouldn't."

"Do it," he insisted. "You don't dare go out there feeling like this."

Kat shook her head, keeping it on the handlebar. Reid kept rubbing her back.

If I took that walk Maria was talking about—dancing with the zombies—

No. Lind and Kat needed him.

Or did they? Without him, without Maria, there'd be no one else to help. Kat wouldn't be forced to work for the witches.

I—I can't do that. Not yet.

He sighed, and went inside to change.

ANOTHER MORNING, another treatment. Reid was gentle with Lindsey as he urged her awake and coaxed more venison down her throat. The meat seemed to give her more strength, but he ended up carrying her to daycare.

She whimpered as they went into the treatment room.

"Buck up," the medtech said. "Looks like you'll not need much more than three more treatments, way you're reacting."

Lind didn't respond to his blandishments but buried her head deeper in Reid's shoulder. He felt her tremble as the infusion started. Even when it was finished, she continued to shake in his arms and refused to leave. The medtech had to carry her outside. Reid watched as he set Lind down on a bench. She immediately lay down, as her friends crowded around her.

"This is all right?" Reid asked.

"As all right as it's going to get," the medtech said, flashing Reid a nearly toothless grin. "Could be worse. She'll be done with treatment this week. Most kids, it takes two weeks, maybe more. How old is she?"

"Nine."

"Small for her age. That's okay. Works better."

"If you say so."

It seemed awful enough to him.

REID KEPT REMEMBERING Lindsey's whimpers as he worked. The witches—Kat among them—chased a flurry of zombies back from the edge of the forest, providing the crew with a brief intermission as they waited to see if they'd need to run.

But the witches prevailed, without casualties—or so he thought.

He'd been working for a few minutes when Mike tapped him on the shoulder. "You're wanted at Witch Central. Dump your load and go."

"Something's happened," Reid gasped to Maria as he emptied his load. "I've got to go to Witch Central."

Maria's lips tightened. "I'll be there as soon as I can."

Reid ran toward Witch headquarters, his imagination concocting all sorts of possibilities.

This can't be happening—God, without Kat—

"What happened?" he demanded of the first witch. "Is Kat all right?"

"Steady, Reid." Another witch came out to join them. "She'll be all right. Just a brush."

"I want to see her."

"Go on back." The witch pulled back the curtain separating the outer room from the back. Kat sat on a table, face paler than usual, holding a cloth to her arm.

"Kat—" Reid gulped. At least she didn't stink of zombie.

"I just—I slipped and cut myself. Not focusing." The sick look on her face sent chills through Reid.

"You're okay. No zombie got you—"

"I'm okay," Kat said. "I'm okay," she repeated, shivering. "It was close, but—"

Reid took her in his arms. Reid wasn't sure of how long they stood there before somebody pushed something into his hand. He looked up, to see Maria, grim-faced.

"Your chit for the day," she said. "Bonus in it for Kat." She patted Kat on the shoulder. "You going to be okay, Sis?"

Kat shook her head. "I can't do this. I can't," she breathed, keeping her voice low so the others couldn't hear them.

Maria caught Reid's eyes. *Later*, she mouthed. "I'll check in on you guys tonight," she said out loud.

"Thanks, Maria. But it shouldn't be necessary—"

"I'll come by later," Maria said, not looking away from Reid.

It was all he could do to keep from shivering at the emptiness in Maria's eyes.

Almost like a zombie.

Both Lindsey and Kat were asleep when Maria came by with a jar of home brew and a joint. Reid and Maria sat on the front step and shared the jar and joint in silence, staring across the narrow passage at the shacks around them.

"She can't go back," Maria said finally, taking the final drag on the joint. "She's not ruthless enough for the witches."

"She said they'd been watching her." Reid took a long pull on the homebrew.

Maria hacked a harsh laugh. "Of course they're watching her! Witch membership is coerced. They can con her into doing it for Lind's sake."

"What are we going to do?" Reid handed Maria the jar.

"If we weren't here, they couldn't force her into the witches."

"So you're saying we should go zombie dancing?"

Maria took a long swig. "I'm not sure—yet."

"Lind has three more treatments," Reid said slowly. "God, what it's doing to her—I can't just leave them, Maria."

"Kat will get at least couple of days off for this injury," Maria said.

Reid exhaled slowly. "Maybe once Lind's treatments are over they'll let her resign."

Maria gave Reid a crooked smile. "Nobody resigns from the witches, Reid. Not unless their families are gone."

Kat stayed home for the next two days while Reid took Lindsey to daycare. The canal work continued steadily with a few feints from the zombies, but no direct attacks. He avoided talking directly to Maria as much as he could. For what it was worth, it seemed she was willing to do the same.

Maybe if we ignore it— Reid kept thinking.

But he knew better.

Reid carried Lindsey to daycare the morning of her last treatment. Instead of sending Lindsey out with the others afterward, the medtech took a blood sample and left them waiting in the room.

Finally, an older woman in medical fatigues came in.

"Congratulations," she said to Lindsey. "It worked."

"So that's it? No more treatments?" Reid asked, hope rising.

The doctor shook her head. "No. She'll need weekly maintenance infusions. In the spring she can go to monthly treatments."

"And after that?"

"She will always need an infusion—possibly six month intervals, more likely two month intervals. We can only keep the syndrome at bay, not completely banish it. Yet."

"Thank you," Reid managed to say through numb lips. He took Lindsey out to join her friends, and kissed her forehead before he left, not daring to look back. He hurried back home to talk to Kat.

She was pulling on her witch fatigues as he burst through the door, her lips and brows drawn down tight in a frightened scowl.

"Kat—not yet—"

"They've called me up," she said, lacing her boots, wrenching the laces more tightly than necessary. "Now that Lind's treatments are done, I'm booked for a three-day tour."

"Kat, you can't—"

"The canal job ends soon. You're not a candidate for the witches. Lind's treatments—"

"Somebody came by while I was with her, didn't they?"

She nodded slowly, looking down at her feet.

"Kat, don't go. Not today. Find an excuse. Something. Anything."

"They know I'm not sick," she said.

Reid gulped. "Then I'll have to do something."

"What?"

"Close your eyes," he commanded, his gut twisting. "I'll hit you, dislocate your shoulder—something. God, Kat, I'm so sorry, this is the only thing I can think of."

"Don't hit me," she said, her voice trembling. "That won't be enough. You'll have to break something—I can't scream, that'll bring people too fast—" She wrenched her shirt off.

"Kat—" he pleaded.

"*Just get it done!*" She jammed the shirt in her mouth and extended her shaking arm, averting her head so she wasn't looking at him.

"I'm sorry—"

Breaking her arm was harder than he thought it would be. He was the one choking back screams as Kat passed out at his feet, tears streaming from his eyes.

"Goodbye, Kat," he breathed, bending to kiss her. He rifled the cabinets for weapons, both the defensive weapons he'd been issued and Kat's witch weapons.

To his surprise, no one was waiting to grab him as he bolted down the alleys. He ignored Mike's call as he ran past his wheelbarrow, looking for Maria.

He slowed as she stood up from her cement spreading, her face tightening as she took in his expression and the weapons arrayed on his belt.

"Let's go zombie dancing," he said.

Maria nodded. She pulled up the shapeless folds of her tunic to show him her weapons.

"I figured today was the day." She dropped her spreader and the two of them carefully navigated the dry walls of the canal. Reid was conscious of the others stopping work to watch them go.

Mike caught up with them.

"Isn't there another way?" he asked.

Reid shook his head. "Look after Kat and Lind for me, will you, please?"

"I will—but Reid—"

"Kat's hurt. She's got a broken arm." Reid blinked hard, the tears coming back to blur his vision. "I can't go back, Mike."

Mike nodded. "I understand." He sighed. "Good hunting. Dance well."

"We'll try," Maria said.

Reid and Maria marched toward the forest. He wondered for one quick moment if Jemmie would be among the zombies.

As they reached the tree line, he and Maria pulled out their guns.

The time to dance was upon them.

THIS IS one of two zombie stories I've written, the only ones I'll probably ever write as zombies really aren't my thing. I got my start writing for small press themed anthologies, and this story showed up in one that received kudos, but was then pulled off the market.

So here it is, again.

14

SO SORRY ABOUT YOUR LOSS

Jenny stared at the card from the plain gray envelope. It bore the image of a flying saucer in a desert setting, with a cuteish, gray-skinned, bug-eyed alien waving in a friendly manner in the foreground.

With Deepest Regrets was curlicued in elaborate cursive purple script at the top, superimposed over part of the saucer.

She scowled, and opened the card. Soft strains of organ music began to pipe from the card. She struggled to make out the inscription inside.

SO SORRY ABOUT YOUR LOSS, the first sentence read, in bright, flashing pink cursive, that was, if anything, more elaborate than the script on the front of the card. WE REGRET THE NECESSARY DEATH OF YOUR DEAR ONE STEVEN. This script was slightly less elaborate, in magenta tones. OUR REGARDS, <~!*&>, EARTH INVASION FORCE.

"Bastards!" Jenny flung the card against the wall. The organ continued to chord on, the notes warped. She stared across the room at it, her nostrils flaring, eyes filling with tears.

Steven's not dead. He can't be—one of our people would tell me first.

A knock sounded on the apartment door. Jenny gulped. The walk to the door took forever. When she opened it, two men wearing the blue and green of the Earth Defense Force stood framed uncomfortably in the doorway, their faces solemn.

"WE'VE GOT to do something about this invasion and soon," the anonymous general said to his attaché. The attaché nodded, whipping out her smartphone to take notes. "This —sending of cards after each battle—it's ridiculous! *They're* contacting the next-of-kin of our casualties before we can officially notify them ourselves, and they're our *enemies!* Isn't there something about that in the Geneva Convention?"

"I'll check," the attaché said. She already knew the answer, but it was better to say she would check. It might give her a couple of minutes to look at social media.

"Make it happen. Soon." The general walked away, his brow furrowed hard, Deep Thoughts clearly passing through his mind.

The attaché headed off for her cubicle.

LUV U 4EVR, her fiancé texted.

She swallowed hard, thinking about his ship hanging in the blackness of space overhead, awaiting the next wave of saucer invaders.

U NO I WILL, she texted back.

JENNY CHOKED BACK HER TEARS, waiting for the baggage carousel to unload the box holding Steven's cremains.

They couldn't even deliver those personally!

Earth Defense Forces were notorious cheapskates, but this had to be the worst part of it.

At last the box rose slowly out of the center of the carousel. It slid gently down the side and bumped against the bottom. Jenny picked it up and started to carry it away, wrapping her arms around the box.

Someone in uniform stopped her. "ID? That yours?"

Blinking back her tears, she flashed the ID. The security guard looked, nodded, and let her pass.

Bastards, she thought as she hurried to the light rail stop. *As if anyone would steal a box of ashes.*

Jenny blinked back more tears.

How soon would it be until she had to vacate their apartment? It was slotted for double plus occupancy, not a single.

When she got home, there was another plain gray envelope in her mail.

This card had a picture of her walking down the street, loaded down with suitcases.

SO SORRY YOU'RE ON THE STREET, this one read, in bright green lettering.

THE FIVE-NOTE INTRO to the newest popular news scandal show echoed throughout the spaceport lobby.

"Breaking news about the alien invasion scandal!" a female voice intoned as the show's logo slowly filled the video screens. The logo faded, replaced by a flashy ad.

"Multiplex! Guaranteed to not just boost those sper-ma-zoa but speed up the gender swimmers you want!"

The colorful animation showed a dancing tadpoleish figure in blue outracing a pink tadpole.

"Boys or girls! Your pick or your money back! Millions of satisfied customers world-wide! That's Multiplex!"

A chorus line of dancing and weaving pink and blue figures faded out, to be briefly replaced by a crying baby with ANOTHER MULTIPLEX SUCCESS!!!!! superimposed over it in flashing pink and blue lettering.

The baby was replaced by a slow fade to a well-dressed male and female chatting with each other behind a retro 70s-era news desk. The female smiled, adjusting her video glasses so the camera caught her eyes even as she scanned the news feed across the lenses.

"Our news tonight!" she bubbled at the camera. "The Alien invasion forces appear to be using greeting cards to harass the families of our brave men and women of the Earth Defense Forces!"

Jenny sat in her new studio apartment, boxes piled around her. She sighed and stared at the box of Steven's cremains. So far, she'd not dared to open the container. The old Harley Davidson tin she'd bought for his ashes waited. But the thought of actually opening the box and moving the ashes was too much to bear.

Have to do it sometime.

Slowly, she ripped open the taped lid of the cardboard box.

Solemn organ chords greeted her as she pulled back the

flaps. The plain gray envelope she'd by now grown to hate rested on top of the box within the shipping box.

With trembling hands, she ripped open the envelope.

SO SORRY BUT WE WEREN'T ABLE TO RETRIEVE YOUR LOVED ONE'S REMAINS, the card blinked in friendly yellow letters that ended with a smiley face.

Jenny screamed and threw the card, then the boxes, across the room.

THE GENERAL MARCHED into his attaché's cubicle, not taking note of her swollen eyes as she stared at the cuteish card with a flying saucer in a desert setting, and a bug-eyed alien waving in a friendly manner in the foreground.

"So what have you found out about those greeting cards?" he asked.

She burst into tears and ran down the hallway screaming.

The general looked after her, raising his eyebrows. Then he noticed the card. He picked it up, eying the front. He opened the card. There was a tiny "pop," and a white puff from the card. The general coughed, choked, then collapsed.

He was quite purple, and it took some time, before anyone noticed his still body lying on the floor.

JENNY'S STILL, bloody body lay in the studio apartment, boxes scattered around her, her fiancé's pistol in her hand.

There was a soft rustle as a card, this time outside of the plain gray envelope, fell through the mail slot in the door.

SO SORRY ABOUT YOUR DAUGHTER'S DEATH, it read.

ANOTHER ONE of those stories from the teaching era that had its origin in a specific event!

Our school secretary was signing yet another card for yet another recognition event—I forget what it was, it was late in the year when the celebratory potlucks happened fast and furious and ended up running into each other.

She looked up and said "I swear, there are greeting cards for just about any occasion!"

And I thought...hmm, what about alien invasion by greeting card?

15
THE NOTICE

For once it wasn't dark and raining when she left work. Yarrow hesitated in the lobby of her office building, surveying the outdoors as she adjusted her coat. There was the slightest hint of gold light to the west that reflected into the street from an upper row of windows on the skyscraper opposite her building. Her fingers itched to seize the warm golden glow and spin it into a bright web to cheer those around her. It was one thing she had done to make Jenny smile even in the darkest political hours.

No, she told herself. Yarrow knew better than to try to weave the light, even to bring joy to others and divert their thoughts from this drab, dreary time. Doing so might trigger her building's wards.

Still, Yarrow leaned against the floor-to-ceiling window and gazed at the golden light before it faded. She savored the glow's cheery warmth, delaying the moment when she would have to pass through the building's wards. She could remember Jenny's smile and hope that she could see this quick glow even in Relocation Camp #5. Thinking about

Jenny helped Yarrow ignore the handful of people who glowered at her.

Witch. Outsider. Yarrow didn't need to hear them speak to know their fear and anger. Their emotions were so palpable that she almost expected to see a second being embodying that fear and anger stalking alongside those who glared at her.

Never mind that during the Change she had healed many of those who now glowered at her. Never mind her small kindnesses to those who were hurting, or how she had defended her coworkers against the Shadows that stalked the city during the Change. She shared the power of the Shadows, even though she was vowed to protect, not destroy. The Censors had declared all witches, all magic, to be dangerous, whether positive or destructive.

The golden light faded. Yarrow heaved a sigh. She tapped the bracelets that controlled her magic to the outside non-work setting, and winced as a dull pressure rose in her sinuses. The world about her darkened. Not as bad as it would be without that fleeting memory of sunglow, or what it would be like if rain accompanied the ever-present wind that was the legacy of the Change. But the throbbing headache grew as Yarrow merged into the hordes exiting the building.

One spiteful part of her wanted to cling close to the woman who sidled away from her as they approached the door, so that she'd get a taste of the pain from the wards. Yarrow dismissed that urge. *Remember your vows,* she told herself. Likely the woman had just been too close to another witch passing through the wards once upon a time. Or another, angrier, witch had passed on her own pain to that woman.

Not that it mattered. Any such rebellious witches were

long gone, enslaved by the Censors before they became powerful enough to become problematic. How long would it be until she fell into the category of *problem witch* along with the disappeared?

Don't think about that, she told herself. *Think about home.* Maybe the trip home would be peaceful and she would have the energy to tell small stories to Carlos and Marisol, Leslie and Maria's kids. It had been a low magic day at work, so perhaps she'd have enough left in her daily allotment to illustrate her stories with the animated creatures the kids loved.

But first she had to get home without incident. Yarrow steeled herself and went through the doorway. Cold fire lanced through her, seeking wrongness, and she bit her lip against it. Sensing no wrongdoing from Yarrow for her day's work, the sharpness of the cold fire faded as she passed through the vestibule and the second door. But the dull throb in her forehead grew stronger as she went outside. This query from the building had hurt more than usual, and the cold wind whispering through the skyscraper canyons didn't help.

Once she reached the bus shelter, Yarrow stood in the yellow-painted rectangle on the pavement outside the shelter labeled WITCHES ONLY. No one came near her. Two middle school-aged boys hissed mocking words at her. She ignored them, knowing the tone too well to make the effort to make sense of the hurtful words. She huddled down into her coat as the damp cold wind whipped around her, relieved when the bus finally pulled up.

The line to get on the bus stretched almost to her rectangle. Yarrow waited as the normals loaded, worrying. The next bus might not reach her stop before curfew, and she'd have to use magic to hide herself and get home safely.

But at last the back door of the bus opened. She slid in and found her customary seat on the steps, next to another woman with restraint bracelets and the witch glyph on her coat. They sat together gingerly, careful not to touch in case their bracelets objected to the contact.

The bus stopped. Yarrow and the other witch stood and pressed against opposite sides of the stairwell as the norms left. One man banged his bag against Yarrow's shins. She bit her lip to keep from giving him the satisfaction of knowing he had caused her pain. He scowled at her.

"—witches," she heard him say as she sunk into herself again. At least she hadn't heard the epithet clearly. Yarrow leaned her head against the stairwell and whispered a tiny *obscure* charm to make her less noticeable. Her bracelets vibrated a warning, sending sharp tingles up and down her arms. Yarrow closed her eyes and breathed through her mouth. A little more pain and a little less magic was tolerable compared to the possibility of *just one more* encounter like that.

She'd be home soon. Safe for another night. She hoped.

And it was still another night without Jenny.

THE STREETLIGHT at her stop had burned out again. Yarrow tensed as she stepped off of the bus, switching from *obscure* to a *scan* charm of equal strength. Sometimes the Censors switched off the light to let anti-witch mobs hunt freely. Prickles of pain radiated from her bracelets as they protested the stronger charm. Yarrow bit her lip to create a counter to that pain. She scanned behind the low brick wall dividing the patio of a condominium complex from the sidewalk, the most likely space for an ambusher to hide.

Nothing. She extended her scan to include the low row of arborvitae lining the foundation of the apartments next to the condos. Nothing. Perhaps the light had legitimately burned out.

Nonetheless, Yarrow remained cautious as she walked two blocks past increasingly shabby apartment buildings until she reached the rundown two-story complex that held her studio. The light being out could also mean that a raid was immanent. But no dangers lurked in the narrow dark courtyard between the two wings of the building.

The main entry door was ajar so that she didn't need to punch her code to get in, a thin thread of light spilling into the dark outside. Yarrow pushed it open, alert. Nothing in the dingy foyer. She stopped at her mailbox. Nothing there, either. Disappointment rose in her. She'd hoped to have a letter from Jenny. It was almost time for the Censors to let her write.

Despite her disappointment, she noticed that the building was far too quiet as she climbed the stairs. No mouth-watering scent of spicy dinner wafting from Abdul and Kareen's apartment down the north wing hallway on the main floor. No kid noise from Maria and Leslie's apartment near the second floor landing. No distant mumbles of TVs from other apartments as she walked to her door. It was as if no one else was at home—which wasn't right. Everyone should be in the building now, comfy and cozy against a world turned alien. She would be the last one home, just in time before the wards locked them down for the night, witches all neatly tucked into their ghetto.

Dread clutched at Yarrow's stomach. *A raid?* If so, then why hadn't she been taken, too? Or had the Censors decided to leave her here, alone, with no protection except her restricted magic against a mob wielding Censor-approved magic?

A yellow sheet of paper on her door heightened her sense of doom. Yarrow detached it with shaking hands. The words splayed across the narrow paper in an incongruously cheerful magenta font.

RELOCATION ORDER

24 HOUR NOTICE.

DO NOT GO TO WORK.

DO NOT LEAVE THE BUILDING

UNTIL NATIONAL SECURITY COMES FOR YOU.

DO NOT WORK MAGIC.

BE PACKED.

NO MORE THAN TWO BAGS.

Yarrow gulped, blinking back tears. So this was it. She crumpled the notice into a tight ball in one hand and unlocked her door, her hands shaking. She slammed the door shut behind her and collapsed on the floor, sobbing in fear and rage.

What good was having the witch gift to help her fellow humans survive the Shadows if those she was supposed to protect turned on her like this? Maybe she should have joined Jenny in her rebellion. Maybe she should have fought the Censors instead of acquiescing to their demands, hoping to stay safe. Cooperation was all for nothing!

But the Witches Council—now the Resistance Council —had held otherwise. Had argued that since witches had helped fight the Shadows, the normals would tolerate them.

That had been before Lafitte and the Censors gained

power, though, playing on the normals fear of magic unconnected to churches. Jenny had refused to play along. She had fought back. And now she was in Relocation Camp #5. Still, she had urged Yarrow to collaborate, to be her eyes and ears on the Council.

What good did it do? Yarrow wondered bitterly. She pushed herself upright, and spotted an envelope on the floor close to the door, her name inscribed on it in fine black calligraphy. *Now what?* She reluctantly picked it up. The envelope was of good quality, the type used for fancy invitations or thank yous. Her heart started to pound harder. Could it be—? The Council used cards like this to communicate. It was easier to authenticate physical cards, and the Censors couldn't monitor them as well as they could electronic communications.

Yarrow dared not get her hopes up too high, even though she felt the tingle of magic within the envelope. She lightly tapped the bright red seal on the back flap. The Censors had been known to use traps like this. But the hope that this was from the Council and not the Censors kept her going. It didn't *feel* like a Censor's trap.

A faint chime sounded. Authentic. A missive from the Resistance Council. Hands shaking, Yarrow broke the seal and took out the card.

DESTROY AFTER READING flashed at the top in bright red letters.

Underneath, in the same fine calligraphy that had been on the envelope, the message continued.

Time is of the essence and the Censors are watching the building. Raid hit at 2 pm today. Got everyone but me, Maria, and the kids. Abdul is dead for certain. We need to free the survivors and your services are required by the Council. Censors won't give you even an hour at home before they come in. Get your things ready and wait for my knock. Destroy this now. "Burn to nothingness."

Leslie
RC-authenticated

"Burn to nothingness," Yarrow repeated the auto-destruct command, staring at the missive as both card and envelope disappeared in a bright flash. Her bracelets jolted sharply but she didn't notice the pain. Leslie? *Leslie* was the Resistance Council lead in the building? Chunky little Leslie with her bright grin? Then again, Leslie was active, with a muscular core that meant she instead of Maria was the one doing their family's share of the heavy work around the apartment complex.

Yarrow rose and yanked her big backpack that held the bag filled with her magical implements and other things she might want should she need to flee in a hurry out of her armoire. Nervousness made her fingers clumsy as she fished for the bag that held her magic supplies. The Council hadn't called upon her to do anything more than her daily job since the Change. She wasn't that powerful a witch and her position as a worker of protective charms for the war effort against the Shadows was a higher priority for her small talents than working for the Resistance. She had turned in enough of her personal magical supplies to throw the Censors off of any suspicions that she was anything other than a submissive, docile witch who would do what they ordered. Even if her girlfriend was Jenny, face of the Resistance.

Her fingers steadied as she pulled out the gold-colored leather back that held her magic supplies. She eased the bag's ties and began her inventory. Her small charms—still potent. The potion vials were full in their stiff leather case, none of the seals broken. Yarrow slipped two ring charms onto her fingers, uncertain why except that they called to her. One held a small vial of consecrated salt. Her athame tingled as she brushed her fingers against its black hilt and the moonstone sigil set within it. She placed it to one side, planning to hang it from her belt once she changed clothing.

Lastly, she pulled out the small velveteen jewelry bag and shook out its contents. The silver wire-wrapped amethyst on a silver chain slid into her hand, her bracelets stinging as the amethyst began to glow. Yarrow shuddered and closed her hand into a fist around the amethyst, embracing the pain from the bracelets instead of rejecting it. Then she hung the amethyst around her neck, ignoring the persistent complaining prickle from her bracelets. She drew a deep, shuddering breath as the amethyst settled between her breasts.

I will be docile no longer, she vowed. Guilt pricked at her. Jenny would not like this.

But Jenny was no longer here. Yarrow quickly changed into jeans. She strapped the sheathed athame on her heavy leather belt, then filled the backpack with the rest of the things she needed to flee.

That done, Yarrow straightened up and looked around the studio. This tiny studio had been home for six months, third place in eighteen months. She paused to finger the three porcelain horses she had managed to bring along until now, all gifts from Jenny. This time she would have to leave them.

Tap-tap. Tap-tap-TAP-tap rattled on the door as she finished tying the laces on her hiking boots. That was clearly not the Censors knocking on the door. But Yarrow was still cautious.

Friend or foe? she queried the amethyst, reaching up with her left hand to clutch it through the wool sweater.

It pulsed warm in her hand. *Friend.*

Yarrow dropped her hand and peered through the spyhole. Leslie stood in front of the door, looking around nervously. Yarrow let her in.

"I'm ready," Yarrow said.

"Good," Leslie gulped. "We have to go. Now. They got Maria and the kids, too!"

Chills gripped Yarrow's gut. "But the kids aren't witches!"

"They're tainted by witch contact," Leslie groaned. "Come on! Let's go!"

Yarrow bent to grab her backpack, something about the tone in Leslie's voice setting her on edge. Coolness radiated from the amethyst, confirming her reaction. *Something not right.*

"I have to check something," she said to Leslie, kneeling next to her backpack, using it to cover her movements as she unsheathed her athame.

The *not-right* feeling grew.

"Hurry up! What could be so important?" Leslie knelt next to Yarrow and the *not-right* sensation became stronger. *But the amethyst said she was safe—no, it said she was a friend.*

Yarrow looked into Leslie's eyes.

"What happened with Maria and the kids?" she asked calmly, reaching up to grasp her amethyst with her left hand as she held the athame hidden.

Friend but not safe came back to her.

"Why are you wasting time?" Leslie grabbed and shook

Yarrow. Yarrow dropped the amethyst and twisted Leslie's right hand behind her back.

"*What happened with Maria and the kids?*" she demanded, touching the point of the athame to the jugular vein in Leslie's neck, feeling nauseated by the aggression. But she had to know.

"Why are you wasting our time with this?" Leslie's voice quavered and for the first time Yarrow noticed that Leslie's bracelets were gone. But there was no flow of power from Leslie like there should be from a witch with no bracelets. Had she ever truly been a witch? Or had the Censors' bracelets been the source of Leslie's magic? Yarrow had heard of such things, but had considered them wild tales. Now she wasn't so sure.

Leslie always pooh-poohed those stories, she remembered.

"What happened to your bracelets?" Yarrow asked, even as the pain radiating from her own bracelets grew stronger. "Why are you in such a hurry?"

Leslie wouldn't meet Yarrow's eyes. "We've got to go. Now!"

Yarrow pressed harder on Leslie's neck. The athame stirred in her hand and nicked Leslie's vein. A bead of blood welled up, then disappeared, sucked up by the athame.

"You betrayed them, didn't you?" Yarrow asked.

"I—I—I didn't mean to!" Leslie stammered. Her eyes widened. "We've got to go! Fast!"

"Why? So you can hand me over to the Censors?" Yarrow delicately drew the point down Leslie's neck, steeling herself for the next move. If Leslie truly was a traitor to the Council—*Traitor's blood will set you free,* the Censor who had bound Yarrow eighteen months ago had sneered. *But good luck in finding one.*

Well, she'd know soon about Leslie.

"Don't. For the love of all that is sacred, *don't,*" Leslie choked, finally now meeting Yarrow's eyes. "If I bring you then they'll let Maria and the kids go."

Don't drink, Yarrow commanded her athame. She scraped some of the trickling blood from Leslie's neck with the athame's edge. She brushed the blood onto both bracelets, then opened the cap on the salt ring, sprinkling the content over the bracelets.

"Unbind," she whispered.

She didn't know whether to be disappointed or elated when the bracelets fell off.

Leslie crumpled up, burying her face in her hands. "I didn't want to do it, Yarrow."

"But you did. Where are they?" The flood of regained power was almost intoxicating, begging her to use magic to coerce Leslie, but Yarrow pushed it back.

Leslie raised her head, sniffling. "I—I don't know. The Censors said they'd exchange them for you at a meeting point."

"And you believed them?" What could she do now? Yarrow didn't know what to think. But even more was wrong. She wasn't a powerful witch. Why would the Censors bring her in like this? Why was *she* worth the effort of having Leslie bring her in specially?

Think, Yarrow, think.

She could find some clues from scanning the notice. Where had she dropped it? Yarrow spotted the crumpled ball of paper. She picked it up, smoothing out the creases, and studied it again. Without the suppression bracelets her magic easily identified the origin of the notice.

Relocation Office #5.

The office affiliated with Jenny's camp. Yarrow pushed harder, touching her athame to the paper, hoping to scry further meaning from the paper in her hand, thinking about Jenny.

The paper caught fire, startling Yarrow into dropping it, but not before she got an image of a manacled, emaciated Jenny yelling obscenities. *Pushed it too hard.* But still—Jenny had managed to project a warning into the notice. *Run, Yarrow, run! For my sake!*

If they catch you, you're the key to Jenny, Yarrow realized. *They can break her if she knows you're a prisoner, too. You have to stay free.*

Leslie darted toward the door and Yarrow grabbed her arm again, yanking her back.

"Ow!" Leslie struggled until Yarrow held the athame to her neck. "Yarrow, by all that is holy, please—in the name of Maria and the kids, *please*."

"Why should I trust you?" Yarrow hissed. Knowing that Jenny's ability to resist was at stake gave her the courage to be angry with Leslie.

"You don't understand," Leslie groaned. "I was just trying to save Maria and the kids."

The athame's hilt didn't change temperature. So a half-truth.

"Where are they?" Yarrow demanded.

"I—I don't know!"

"Where were you taking me?"

Leslie sniffled. Yarrow pressed harder with the athame.

"The North Square!" Leslie finally screamed.

The athame cooled in Yarrow's hand. *Lie.* Yarrow sighed. She didn't have time for this. If Leslie had shown up this quickly, then the Censors wouldn't be far behind. She had to leave. Alone. She couldn't risk being caught now, not when Jenny had found the means to warn her.

Where will I go? She'd be out after witches' curfew, with

a backpack that would identify her as a fugitive. Couldn't be helped. She fingered her other ring. It should be able to guide her to a safe place for tonight.

But first she had to deal with Leslie. Yarrow swallowed hard, then drew on her now freed magic.

"Hold," she breathed. Leslie gulped for air and strained to rise as Yarrow got up but could do no more than flex against invisible restraints. Yarrow picked up her discarded bracelets, studying them. She fished out a vial of magic transformation dust from her magic bag, and a couple of twist-ties from the bottom of the backpack. She wove the twist-ties between the two bracelets, then ran her fingers along them, whispering the charm she had used to make bindings against the Shadows. The ties swelled into a solid chain linking the bracelets. Lastly, she shook a pinch of dust from the vial over them.

Yarrow fastened Leslie's wrists behind her back. Then she used an extra blouse and more dust plus the binding charm to create another restraint on Leslie's ankles.

That done, Yarrow sighed.

She shrugged on a coat, then the backpack. "Forget I was ever here," she commanded the studio and Leslie, scattering the last of that vial's dust over Leslie and around the studio. Then she trudged back down the hallway to the stairs. Instead of going out the front, Yarrow continued to the basement, and let herself out the back door, hesitating before climbing up the stairwell.

Where to now? Try to rescue Maria and the kids, maybe even try to rescue Jenny?

No. Her magic wasn't that strong, and she risked being captured and used to break Jenny's will.

And Jenny had ordered her not to try to do that before she had been taken.

If you ever get free, run. Run for the border. I will know you've gone, and that will set me free, too.

Yarrow wanted to go back. She wanted to save Jenny, save Maria and the kids. But oh, she had promised Jenny. Yarrow wrapped her hand around the amethyst again.

I am free, Jenny.

The stone warmed in her hand. *Run free. Run free and testify to what we endure now.*

I will, she promised. Then she climbed up the stairwell and headed down the alleyway.

She had to find a place for tonight. Then tomorrow, early, before her absence was discovered, she'd slip down to the river to join other wanderers. Drift with them to the frontier, hiding her magic until she had the chance to cross the border—and hope that the curse of the Censors had not spread further.

For you, Jenny, she vowed. *For you and for freedom.*

She hoped it would work.

It had to work, for all their sakes.

Yes, Alma drew me in for a second anthology.

She's good at that.

"The Notice" has some elements in common with the world in my BEATING THE APOCALYPSE book—in part, much of the setting is inspired by downtown Portland, Oregon.

GNOMES AND SPRITES

16

FAMILY HISTORY

"Are you coming to the Writing SF Outside camp during Solstice?" Static garbled Ellie's voice as Nan entered the utility room. "It's become a joke about how you never seem to get there. It's been what, three years?"

Nan put the cellphone on speaker and set it on the dryer. "I'm going to try. But I can't help it if I blow a tire." She ignored the six-inch tall, colorfully-clad garden gnome that appeared on the top of the dryer. It fixed her with a disapproving glare as it pushed up the drooping point of its red cap.

"Or can't get a day off, or hubby gets sick, or, or, or," Ellie laughed. "Almost seems like you don't want to join us."

The *thing* swiped at the phone. Nan snatched the cell out of its way so that the beast fell into the empty clothes-basket. She put the phone back on the dryer.

"Ellie, I *want* to be there. I need to work on the new novel. I just don't know if I can spend the day in the woods writing."

Jane had been the perfect housewife for Harry, a transient thought chided her.

Not her thought. And Harry had never made such a statement about his ex-wife.

Had he?

"Plus, I have to get caught up with housekeeping," Nan added.

The gnome nodded approvingly, baring its needle-sharp fangs in a grin before leaping back onto the dryer.

You want to be like Jane.

"Like Harry really cares about housework! Come camp with us. You know Don always brings extra tents and sleeping bags. Kevin's setting up a *big* telescope for stargazing. Maybe if you commit to the whole weekend instead of one day, you'll make it. Gives you forty-eight hours to get there instead of twelve."

"Well—I could be persuaded." Nan slammed the lid down on the washer.

After all, Jane had divorced Harry, no matter what that monstrous *beast* tried to claim.

Harry wanted *her.* Nan. The writer. The creator of fantastic worlds. Not Nan the housewife.

The gnome shook its head at her. *You want to be more like Jane.* The thought buzzed around her brain like an errant housefly.

"But isn't it supposed to rain?" Nan continued.

The gnome beamed at her. *Good girl. Like Jane.*

"Really, Nan." She could almost hear Ellie rolling her eyes. "This is Oregon. You aren't going to melt in a little summer rain. Besides, the campground's on the other side of the Cascades."

"I want to work on my novel," Nan said wistfully.

"Then do it!"

The gnome scowled at her. *Be like Jane.*

I'm tired of you. Nan snapped it on the head with her middle finger. The gnome caught her finger with one sharp fang. "Ow!"

"You okay?"

"Just caught my hand on something." The gnome knocked the cellphone off the dryer. She grasped the cell before it hit the floor. The gnome flexed its hands, revealing sharp, talon-like claws. Nan turned her back on it, resolve hardening. *I need to get this next book done.* "I can't make it for the weekend, Ellie. But I *will* be there on Saturday."

The phone cut out. The gnome appeared in the hallway, blocking Nan's path. *You shall not go. Be like Jane.* It grabbed her foot and tried to gnaw her ankle.

Nan sighed. *If I didn't write this sort of thing for a living, I'd think I was losing my mind.*

Careful research had told her that when the creature got like this, lying was the only means to make it go away temporarily. She put both hands behind her back and crossed index and middle fingers. Crossing fingers was important. It worked for brief lies like this one.

"All right," she conceded, making certain that her fingers were firmly crossed. The slightest slippage would betray her. "I'll stay home and keep you company. I'll be like Jane."

And no more of this writing stuff?

"That I won't promise."

The gnome flashed its teeth at her. But it released its hold on her ankle and trotted down the hallway. Nan stuck her tongue out at it, confident that it didn't see her.

One way or another she would break free from its bondage.

Maybe I'll write a story about it at the gathering.

"Isn't it time for the Writing SF Outside campout again?" Harry asked over dinner.

Nan froze. She looked around for any hint of the gnome's presence. It usually didn't come out when Harry was around, but for him to talk about her writing—that could change things.

"I don't know," she said, keeping her voice low. "After the car problems last year, and your collapse at work, it's a little scary to think about going."

"Ellie called me." Harry frowned at her. "She seemed to think it was *me* that keeps you from going. Like I'd do that! I love your writing. I can't wait for this next book. I'd hate to think I was the reason you weren't getting it done."

Nan sighed. "No, it's not you."

Be like Jane, a faint thought whispered in her ear. Was that a telltale wisp of a sagging red cap peeking around the corner?

Harry is here. Let's take a chance. See if that thing attacks me when he's around.

"But it does seem odd that things just keep happening around the time of SF Outside," she continued.

"Would it help if I went this time?"

"It would make a difference if the fan belt breaks like it did last year," Nan said.

"Then I'll come too."

Be like Jane. The whisper of thought grew stronger.

It's here. But where?

"Won't you be bored?"

"I can always read." Harry's eyes widened and he lunged across the table, landing hard on its top.

"What the—!" Nan ducked; arms raised to protect her head as she fell to the floor.

The gnome flailed and kicked at Harry as he held it at arm's length. "I thought I was rid of you," Harry snarled. "Nan. Is this why you haven't gone to SF Outside the last three years?"

"Yes," Nan croaked. "I first saw it at that old ranch outside of Shaniko that we stayed at instead of the campground. It followed me home. And it keeps telling me to be like Jane."

"Do you remember the ranch owner's name?"

"Spencer, I think."

"Damn it," Henry growled. "Family history coming back to haunt me. The Boleyn family curse. Pull that cap off, would you? If this damn Red Cap gets loose now, God above only know what it'll do, riled as it is."

His matter-of-fact tone chilled Nan. "How do you know about these things?" She ventured close. The gnome's wild eyes fixed on her. It strained against Harry's hands as she tentatively reached for the cap.

"Make it quick, for God's sake, Nan! I thought I buried the damn thing years ago. Just grab the cap!"

Nan steeled herself. She grabbed the gnome's cap, revealing bloodstained white hair. The gnome wailed. It shifted from the malignant live parody of a ceramic garden gnome to a knobby, ill-proportioned figure garbed in gray, with rusty metal boots and long claws, eyes bulging from its small head as it stabbed at Harry with a small pike.

"What the—?" Nan dropped the cap as she realized the red coloring was coming off on her fingers.

"Quickly now," Harry said. "While you still have the blood on your fingers. Pull its pike. Then I can bind it temporarily."

"That's blood?" Her stomach turned.

"For the love of heaven, Nan, just do it before that blood dries!"

The urgency in his tone jerked her into action. Nan swiped at the pike and missed. Harry muttered under his breath as the gnome's keening turned to cackling. She tried again and knocked the pike free. Her fingertips burned from the contact and she rubbed them together to ease the pain.

"*In nomine Patris, et fili, et Spiritus Sancti,*" Harry chanted, his eyes wide and wild. The gnome whimpered, solidifying. "Now get a paper bag, Nan, quickly. No, two bags. One for the hat and pike, too. Don't wipe the blood yet."

"How am I going to clean this up?" Nan grabbed two big paper sacks from the shelf they stored them and returned to Harry. Harry dropped the stilled gnome into the bigger one and rolled the top down.

"We'll do it together, with salt. Make crosses with the cap's blood on all four sides," he directed, lifting the sack. "No, five, don't forget the bottom."

Nan shakily drew the crosses. "Harry, what is this?"

"I'll explain when we're done. Quickly. Wrap the pike in the cap, and then mark that bag like this one. Then hold the bag until the blood crosses have dried on the bottom. That's important. Otherwise, the thing can get its tools. We can't have that."

"I didn't think gnomes were supposed to be mean," she said.

"It's not a gnome." Harry inspected the crosses on the bottom of his bag. He sighed with relief. "There's room in the freezer. Put both in."

"What is it and why did you call it a Boleyn family curse? Why does it want me to be like Jane?"

Harry carefully placed both sacks in the freezer, stacking frozen vegetables between them.

"It's a Red Cap," he said. "And the family history claims that it's the curse that doomed Anne Boleyn and has haunted her relatives ever since. I bet Jane woke it up—something she would do know how to do, her and her witchy friends. She threatened to do it three years ago, just before our wedding, when her marital support ended, and she tried to ask for a new settlement."

"If Jane sent this, then how are we going to get rid of it?"

Harry shook his head. "Nan, I don't know what else to do."

"I know. SF Outside. Marsha writes about brownies and gnomes. If not, then Ellie or Chris may know something. They write enough fantasy."

"And Terry knows fantasy roleplaying game lore. Nan, one way or another, we'll get our friends to help us!"

"But you're sure we can keep it confined?"

"We have to keep it cold," Harry said. "The Red Cap's power will fade as its cap freezes, and I think the freezer could dry it up. That slows it down, but unfortunately won't kill it."

"The forecast is for cold and rain this weekend. Typical Oregon summer solstice."

"Perfect!" Harry gingerly hugged Nan, not touching her with his hands. "And now, let's clean up. Luckily, I kept a small vial of holy water around that Mom left, just in case the last exorcism didn't work."

"Holy water?"

"Religious artifacts—frequently Christian, but any other faith will do—help keep the Red Cap contained." He guided her to the sink. "Wait here."

Nan stared out the kitchen window as she held her hands awkwardly over the sink. Harry returned with a small cork-stoppered glass bottle.

"Why didn't you tell me about the curse?" she asked Harry as he shook salt over her hands, then followed with delicate dribbles of holy water.

"I thought it was gone from my life, along with Jane." Harry kept his eyes on her hands as he rubbed her fingers.

Nan shook her head. "Henry Thomas Boleyn, just what on earth are you playing with? Next you'll be telling me that this is a result of some deal Anne Boleyn made to marry Henry the Eighth."

Harry finished washing Nan's fingers and he reached for a towel. He carefully dried Nan's fingers, focusing on her hands rather than looking up at her.

"It's not that, exactly."

"Then what?"

"Anne made a deal with a Red Cap to strike back at Cardinal Wolsey for breaking up her love match with Harry Percy, before her involvement with Henry." His hands tightened on her fingers. "She got her revenge on Wolsey, but when it came time for her to pay her part of the deal, she refused. Nan, what's it been asking of you?"

"To give up my writing. To stay here and keep it company."

Harry closed his eyes and tightened his lips. Then he opened them again, shaking his head. "Jane helped me banish it the first time. She would know the name, she would know how to revive it, she would know how to target you. She knew I took pride in your writing." He straightened. "All right. I'm off to get some dry ice. That should keep everything under control. Why don't you let Ellie know we have a puzzle for the group to consider? Be careful about the details, don't talk too much about it on the phone."

"Why?"

Harry flushed again. "Jane's brothers. They're hackers. They know about Red Caps and the curse."

"I'll tell Ellie we're bringing a supernatural puzzle story to work out."

"That should work." Harry kissed Nan on the forehead. "I'm off to get some dry ice."

"I'll pack the camping gear. You might want to get disposable coolers for—the thing and its tools."

"Good idea. I don't want any of its taint in our good cooler!"

Harry left, and Nan went out to the garage, pulling out the camping gear with a lighter heart than she had for ages.

"THAT IS one hell of a writer's block story." Terry frowned at the Styrofoam coolers that Harry had carefully placed at the edge of the campsite's clearing. He had secured each cooler with bungee cords, putting the Red Cap in one and the hat and pike in the other. "You seriously don't want that thing getting out, do you?"

"My family's dealt with it for many generations—and you've not met my ex-wife. She'd revive Robin Redcap if she thought it would get Nan out of my life," Harry said.

"There was something weird about that Spencer Ranch." Ellie's voice quavered. "The place felt weird and scary. Like my characters were coming alive. I still can't look at the piece I wrote that weekend."

"Me too," Gene said. "It *was* odd that we could not get

any reservations for this campground that year. I've never had any problems since then."

"What do we do about this—thing?" Nan asked. "I don't want it haunting me forever."

Marsha scowled thoughtfully at her laptop. "Let me fire up my hotspot and see what I can research. Traditionally, reading from the Bible banished a Red Cap."

Harry shook his head. "Getting rid of this one requires more than that. Especially with my ex-wife involved. She— likes to play with witchcraft."

"I'm going to look up Robin Redcap and William de Soulis," Marsha muttered. "I remember that story."

Nan shivered at the mention of William de Soulis. Even though she didn't know the name, it sent a chill through her. "Who was he?"

"He was the master of the most infamous Red Cap. Robin Redcap was de Soulis's familiar. De Soulis was killed by being bound in a specially forged chain to control his magic, then wrapped in a sheet of lead and boiled." Harry paused. "De Soulis is another of my ancestors. One of his descendants may have aided Anne in calling up Robin Redcap, to wreak her vengeance on Wolsey."

"Great family history you've got there, Harry," Marsha muttered.

Nan ignored their continued discussion, looking around at the forest edges, a niggling urge to write pulling at her. She opened her laptop and the story she had been drafting, whenever the Red Cap had given her a moment of peace.

Nothing happened. No unexpected jolts of electricity, no Red Cap glaring at her from the screen. Nan went back a couple of pages and began to edit, swiftly getting back into the flow of the story.

"Nan. NAN!" Marsha's shout broke the trance.

Nan looked up, surprised. She glanced at the word count. Nearly a thousand words in the last half hour.

"I'm sorry to break into your writing," Marsha continued. "I have a solution. We have to work quickly to be ready by dusk."

Nan saved her work. It felt good to be writing again— but if this worked, then she would be able to write all the time. Well worth the interruption.

By NIGHTFALL they had assembled all the pieces. Gene and Harry built the fire high. Ellie drove to the little country store five miles down the road and returned with three two-pound bags of pickling salt, jars of rosemary and thyme, and a tin of alum.

Marsha heated a kettle of water on the camp stove. "This is probably overkill. But since salt and holy water didn't keep this thing gone, we'll go with a stronger astringent solution. Alum is supposed to protect you from negativity and ill wishes. We'll treat the cap and pike with that before we burn it."

"And then what?" Nan asked.

"Then, if the Red Cap is still in solid form, we break it." Marsha nodded at Terry. "He brought a splitting maul for camp wood. We smash the bag with the Red Cap in it on a tarp, scatter salt over all the pieces, then dump it into the fire as well."

"And if it's not in solid form?"

"Then we improvise. I wrote down Latin verses for everyone to quote at it. I hope we don't need to go that far. Ellie, the alum?"

As Marsha stirred the alum into the boiling water,

Harry brought the smaller cooler over. He delicately retrieved the bag inside it, and dumped both cap and pike into the boiling water. A loud screech blurted from the other cooler. It rocked back and forth.

The screech faded into keening as the water turned red. Marsha lifted the kettle off of the stove and carried it to the fire.

"You need to be the one to burn it," she said to Nan. "Use a stick to pull the cap out, then drop cap and stick into the flames."

Nan took the stick that Harry handed her and poked through the blood-red water until she firmly hooked the cap. As she pulled it out of the water, she gasped. The cap had turned pale white, tendrils of smoke rising from it. It stank of rot and corruption. Nan plugged her nose with her free hand.

"Get-that-into-the-fire," Marsha gasped. She clutched the kettle as it vibrated and wiggled.

Nan dropped the cap, stick and all, into the fire. The flames leapt higher and the keening grew louder, backed by the baying of something canine. Not coyotes. Not dogs.

Harry looked around nervously. "Are there wolves around here?"

"Not supposed to be," Gene said tightly.

"Damn. Jane and her brothers are near."

"What, are they werewolves?" Marsha scowled at him.

"No. But they keep wolf hybrids."

"Well, let's finish this before they show up." Marsha put a bag of salt into Nan's hands. "Make a circle on the tarp." She glanced at Terry, clutching the maul. "You ready?"

Terry nodded.

"How big a circle?" Nan asked.

"Big enough to enclose the Red Cap's sack."

"All right." Nan carefully poured a thick circle of salt, using the first bag and part of the second. Harry brought the other cooler over. He grabbed the sack out of the cooler and dropped it into the middle of the salt circle. High-pitched wails echoed from it.

"Now!" Marsha snapped. She threw the rest of the alum over the sack. The wails stopped.

Terry brought the maul's broad end down on the sack. By the seventh strike, it lay flat.

Nan poured the rest of the second bag of salt over the sack, hands shaking hard. She ripped open the third bag.

"Just what do you think you're doing?" Harry's ex-wife Jane strode into the clearing, flanked by her two brothers, who restrained two large wolves on heavy leads.

"Why did you revive Robin Redcap, Jane?" Harry demanded "You know how evil it is. You got rid of it in the first place."

She scowled at him. "I banished him to preserve our future. Then you left me for Nan."

"What? *You* left *me*. You had your career and your lover, and you told me that I blocked your way. You left me. Nan didn't come on the scene until the divorce was final, so don't blame her!"

"Blame her? She made you happy. You weren't supposed to be happy after I left. Not find your mousy Nan who lives in her own head. You were supposed to wait for me to come back when I got bored!" Jane laughed. It grated on Nan's nerves like huge fingernails on a gigantic blackboard.

Without thinking, Nan hurled the rest of the salt at Jane.

Teach you to make fun of me!

Jane screamed as the salt touched her skin, wrinkles

forming on her face and arms as she shrank into a female Red Cap. She dove at Marsha, who splashed her with bloody water from the roiling kettle. Jane's brothers backed away from the fire as Jane screeched again, their wolves whimpering and whining. She spread her arms wide and transformed into a bat-like creature. Men and wolves both ran. The bat dove at the flattened bag on the tarp. Nan threw a handful of dust and salt at the bat. It chittered, then flew off after her brothers.

The bag burst into flames. Nan joined the others in grabbing shovels to beat the flames back. Once the fire reached the salt circle Nan had made, it winked out. Harry, Nan, Ellie, and Terry gathered up the tarp and dumped its contents on the fire.

Marsha still wrestled with the kettle. "I can't hold it for much longer!"

"The pike!" Harry said. "Pour it into the fire!"

"The water will put it out!" Gene said.

"Not if we pour white gas on the fire!"

"You're nuts!"

Harry grabbed a paper cup and filled it with white gas. "This will be safe. Dump it, then get back. Quickly."

Marsha nodded. She dumped the kettle, water and all, into the flames, then scrambled back as a foul stench arose from the smoldering ashes. Harry threw the cup of white gas on the fire. It exploded with a loud WHOOSH. As the flames died down, Harry tossed first one cooler, then the other, on them.

Nan lost track of how long they hung back from the fire. It wasn't until the stink started to fade that she relaxed, thinking about that story she had been working on.

"Is that it?" Nan asked. Ideas flooded through her imagination, as if a giant dam had broken.

"How do you feel now?" Harry asked.

"I want to write," she told him. "I want to write until I drop tonight. So many ideas."

His smile sent warm quavers throughout her body, and she almost wanted to drag him off into their tent.

Almost. The words saturating her thoughts were more compelling.

She picked up her laptop. "If anyone wants me, I'll be on the writing side of camp."

Harry kissed her. "Go write. I'll be here when you're ready to take a break."

"Thank you," she murmured.

"I married a writer, not a housewife. I'm glad to see the writer's back. Go. Write."

"I will." Before long, Nan's fingers flew over the keyboard, barely able to keep up with the flow of her thoughts.

God, she'd missed writing.

Worst writer's block ever. She hoped she never had to deal with it again.

I DON'T USUALLY WRITE about creatures from European mythology. It's just not my thing—but nonetheless, I had a period where I wrote a few stories.

And yes, I did have tire problems driving to an outside writing retreat one year.

17

SAFE HAVEN

"That fireplace absolutely *has* to go."

Dorakie the house sprite shuddered as the young woman stood in front of the opening to her den in the fireplace stones. Surely this woman wasn't going to take away Dorakie's home? Bad enough that her First Ashes wouldn't let her move to a new house with Harriet and Liz, her best people ever, but now she would lose her reason for staying here?

"Brittany, it's *so* nicely retro." A man joined the woman. "And if we pull that fireplace out, how are we going to match the floors?"

"Oh Jacob," Brittany sighed. "What if Ethan or Ava hit their heads on these rocks? This hearth is going to be so hard to baby proof. Matching the floor is going to be easy in comparison—I don't like that shade of wood, anyway."

"Brit, it won't be that long that we have to worry. We could use baby gates."

"This house is just too small to shut the kids out of the one big space for family."

"You *did* want to buy this place," Jacob said.

"For the location! We'll triple our money in five years." Brittany snorted. "That fireplace goes. Now. The kitchen."

Dorakie shivered as Brittany's heels clacked away from the fireplace. *They're getting rid of my hearth!* She clutched at the little bag in her apron pocket. What was she going to do without her hearth? She'd be homeless!

Sharp hot pinpricks tingled over her arms. Dorakie grabbed the hilt of her needle sword and crept close to the entrance of her den.

"Heh! Thought I smelled a resident sprite!" a gruff voice growled just out of her sight. "And in the fireplace no less."

"This is still my place!" Dorakie hissed through her crack. "I swear it by my First Ashes!"

"Not for long it's yours," the invading kobold grumbled. "First Ashes don't count if the hearth is destroyed. I, Walther, claim this home for myself and my people. Time you were going, little house sprite! I'll dig you out!" Clack! A rock hammer rattled against her entryway.

"No!" Dorakie grabbed her the pouch of ashes in her apron pocket. "You can't get rid of me that easily!" Where was the fireplace stone she kept loosely mortared for occasions like this? She whispered an invisibility spell complete with a benediction to She Who Tends and darted past Walther, scampering up the fireplace stones. Walther sniffed, suspicious, but kept staring at the crack leading to her den.

Where is that rock? Dorakie pulled on the memory of its latest near-fall to help her locate it. Harriet had jumped, startled, when she knocked the rock loose while maneuvering a table past the fireplace. *So it's head-high.* Dorakie had deflected the stone so that it landed next to Harriet's foot without smacking the table. *That was lucky,* Harriet had said, lips pressed together thoughtfully as she stared at the fireplace. The next day she had set up a shrine near the hearth with tasty sweet snacks. The dollop of honey on a biscuit had charged Dorakie's strength for days. The gods in the shrine had not objected when she helped herself, and she was always careful to share with them.

There. The stone shifted under her hand. She tapped the rock with her finger. It slipped free and Dorakie hurled it at Walther.

"Ouch!" Walther yelled, falling with a loud THUMP and a racket of breaking metal.

He lay still and silent.

Dorakie took a deep breath as she waited for him to move, tapping her fingertips three times against the fireplace in sequence, thumb, finger, finger. Still nothing.

She'd have to check. Shivering with fear, she pulled the bag of ashes from her pocket and kissed it for strength. On a whim, she pinched about half the ash from her bag and sprinkled it over her head for more strength. Then she tucked it safely away, planning to creep past Walther and back into her den.

"Got you!" Walther roared, seizing her. Dorakie bit his arm. He yelped and pulled free. She ducked away, dancing out of reach. Her stone had left a jagged tear across his bulbous face and his rock hammer lay shattered. *Thank you, Harriet, for the memory of that blessed honey,* she thought. Without it she would not have had the strength to break his hammer.

But he was much taller and heavier than she, twice her height and easily three times her span. Even with the magic in her ashes this would be a difficult battle.

"For my hearth!" Dorakie charged him, brandishing her needle sword. She danced in close to Walther and jabbed him, capering away before he could grab her. Perhaps she could lead him out across the threshold and raise the *boundaries* spell to lock him out.

Walther was too quick. He seized her by the neck, one huge hand thrusting into her apron to grab for her ashes.

"In the name of She Who Tends!" she shrieked, and thrust her needle deep into his gut.

He bellowed and let go of her, chanting a healing spell. She stabbed at him again, forcing him back. She would *make* him go away, *make* him cross that threshold.

Walther ducked under her sword. He grabbed her wrist and twisted her arm up behind her back. He planted one knee hard on her back while his stubby finger poked into her apron pockets.

"Let. Her. Go," someone commanded. Walther's knee kept pressing on her back and his fingers fumbled over her ash pouch. Dorakie growled and squirmed. Then something yanked him off of her back. She rolled to her side. *Where were her ashes?* Frantically, she fumbled in her pocket. The ash bag warmed to her touch. *Safe.* But it felt smaller than it had before. She must have used more than she had thought to augment her strength.

Assured her ashes were safe, she looked at her rescuer. Walther backed away from yet another sprite, this one between Walther and Dorakie in size. He wore a green tunic with brown breeches, his angular, knobby arms reminding Dorakie of the old, wizened apple tree outside the cottage.

"She has no rights here!" Walther blustered. "My people are moving into the house. I'm taking over." He glowered at Dorakie. "You have three days to get out. Then I'm taking over."

"But I have First Ashes," Dorakie whimpered.

Walther snorted. "And my people are taking out the hearth! You can't take over the oil furnace's chimney because they're replacing that, too, and oil chimneys are MINE."

"She Who Tends will think otherwise," Dorakie answered.

"He's right," the other sprite said. "You have ties elsewhere, which is why I have something to take up with YOU." He pointed at Dorakie. "I can't connect with my new people! You and your ashes are all over my new people's things! I can't find the right balance because of YOU. They keep looking for their wedding sampler. So I came back here to find YOU, because I think YOU know where it is and that's what we need for balance!"

"They're MY people!" Dorakie snapped.

"They don't live here anymore," Walther interjected.

"Shut UP!" both Dorakie and the strange sprite shouted at him. "This is NOT your business!"

"She is intruding on my people's house! She claims First Ashes—well, my people intend to get rid of this—this—thing!" Walther waved at the fireplace, scowling. "She has no rights here!"

"They can't be your people any more if your hearth is here and you didn't go with them," the strange sprite said to Dorakie. "The wedding sampler. If I bring it back I can bond with them. Where is it?"

"I won't tell you," Dorakie said, stiffening her chin.

He pounced on her. Quicker than Walther with thinner and longer, more agile fingers, he extracted the pouch from her apron. Before she could cry out he ripped the pouch open and threw the ashes on her.

"Ashes, ashes, show me the key to her people's hearts," the strange sprite chanted.

"No," Dorakie groaned as light radiated from her den. "My ashes. My people!"

"You left enough of your ashes in their things that I could turn them to my use," the strange sprite said. He canted his head sideways to study her. "You really are a minor sprite, aren't you? The smallest of sprites. Not very strong."

"Strong enough to care for my people!" Dorakie blinked back angry tears.

"But not strong enough to overcome First Ashes and leave with them. Poor little sprite."

She flinched at the pity in his voice. "I have my place."

"*Had* your place," Walther sneered.

"And now their key is mine," the strange sprite said. He gestured, and the sampler wiggled through the crack to fly into his hand. "Perhaps now I can go inside from my tree." He tucked it under a flap of his brown jacket.

"But what about me?" Dorakie whimpered. Already she felt diminished, shrinking in size in comparison to Walther and the strange sprite.

"Go. Now." Walther growled. A dog barked outside while two children screamed happily. All three sprites flinched.

The strange sprite picked her up. "Little one, I will set you outside in a safe place."

"But what about my things?" She couldn't help sniveling as tears blurred her vision.

"Wild wood sprites have no need of house things," the strange sprite said. "We need to leave now, before the *dog* gets here." The world flowed about them, and Dorakie found herself outside, bobbing behind the strange sprite as he clung to her hand.

At last he drug her up a tree to a fork with a small cavity in it. "This cavity is enough to serve you as a home." He hesitated, and then pulled several threads free from the sampler's fabric. "Here. They can spare this. Keep it as a memory."

"I don't want to be a tree sprite!" she cried out.

But he was gone, and darkness was beginning to fall. She needed shelter, now, before the wild things of the night caught her. She hadn't been inside so long as to forget about basic survival. Heartsick though she was, Dorakie wrapped the threads from the sampler into a tiny ball and tucked it into her apron's pocket. Then she crawled into the tree's core, scrambling up high inside the small rotten cavity just beginning to form inside the bigger branch of the fork. She found a couple of grubs and an ant to eat before she wrapped as much of herself as she could into her apron.

The grubs and ant weren't as tasty as that sweet morsel of honey and biscuit had been.

DORAKIE DIDN'T WANT to venture out of the tiny hollow the next morning. But the tree's distress at the arrival of more ants put her to work fighting them off, then weaving a protective shield made of spider silk for the tree. To her surprise, the skills she had learned from evicting destroying intruders from the cottage also worked for the tree.

In return, the tree freely gave her some sap. Between that and the bodies of the ants, Dorakie was able to eat enough to give her the strength to finish the needed tree repairs, cleaning the rot and purging the fungus that had threatened to overtake it. The tree gave her leaves and moss to create a bed. By mid-morning, she had made herself a small den in the tree's hollow.

Now what? She should forage for more food and make herself a warmer bed. But she was sore from yesterday's battle with Walther and heartsick at the loss of her hearth. Dorakie decided to sit in the weak winter sun and think about what to do next.

"R-row," a familiar cat voice chirped at the foot of the tree. "R-r-row." Dorakie looked. A gray tabby crouched below, great green eyes fixed on a sparrow perched on one of her tree's branches. Smoky, one of Liz and Harriet's cats. An indoor cat who didn't know how to survive outside.

But Smoky never escaped when Dorakie was there. She listened to Dorakie's boundaries. The new sprite had failed them in this, and the *boundaries* spell was one of Dorakie's strengths.

Maybe this was her way back to her people. Dorakie wrapped the sampler threads around both hands. Unlike Liz and Harriet's other cat, Ginger, Smoky could be influenced by a smart sprite. Dorakie had snitched rides around the house on Smoky before. With the sampler threads, she could guide Smoky back to the house and perhaps even inside before that other sprite found her. Then she'd have the right of return because she had done the household a favor. That other sprite would be bound by She Who Tends's rules about favors and obligations.

She just had to find a way to get onto Smoky.

"R-rrow," Smoky chirped again. She stretched her declawed paws up the tree to try to climb. "R-rrrrow," she grumbled louder.

Bit by small bit Dorakie crept down the tree. She didn't want to spook Smoky.

"Rrow?" Smoky's frustrated chatter changed to curiosity. She ambled around the trunk. Dorakie leapt from the trunk to Smoky's back. Smoky flinched and hissed, then ran away from the tree. Dorakie clung tight to Smoky's collar, hoping that they didn't attract a *dog's* attention or anything worse.

Home, she thought hard to the sampler threads. *Bring me home.*

The thread tugged at her right hand. She pressed it against Smoky's head. Smoky responded, just like she had in the house, slowing from a panicked run to a steady, ground-covering, jog as she remembered the cues Dorakie had taught her.

They had trotted for what seemed to be ages, following the pull of the sampler threads, when a chorus of barks started up behind them. Dorakie urged Smoky into a run. She didn't have to work hard to persuade the cat to go faster. Smoky bounded along faster than she would usually run, but the baying *dogs*—plural—drew closer.

They approached a white picket fence surrounding a larger cottage with a lovely garden outside of it. Smoky flattened herself to slide under a Smoky-sized gap in the fence. Dorakie clung tight to keep from being scraped off.

The sampler threads burned warm in her hand. They had reached Liz and Harriet's new home. Smoky trotted around the back of the house purposefully. She shinnied through a small gap in a big cage of finely woven wire which held cat trees and a patch of grass as well as a cat box. Smoky ignored all that and slid through a pet door to go inside the house.

"There you are." The other sprite, He Who Had Stolen

Her Place, growled at Smoky. "What am I going to do with you? Fortunate for both of us that our people hadn't found out you were gone yet."

"Haven't you made the *boundaries* spell?" Dorakie asked. She let go of Smoky's collar and slid off the cat's back, standing tall and proud. "Otherwise Smoky keeps getting out."

He Who Had Stolen Her Place frowned and squinted at Dorakie. "Oh. *You* again."

"And I claim right of return for bringing Smoky back," Dorakie countered. "She never escaped when *I* was in charge of the house."

"But, but," he stammered.

"Don't you know the *boundaries* spell?" Dorakie studied He Who Had Stolen Her Place more carefully than she had yesterday. He looked exhausted. "Every house sprite knows the *boundaries* spell. How would you keep creatures like Smoky in and the ants and termites out?"

"We don't need the—what did you call that spell? The *bound*—what spell?"

"*Boundaries*," Dorakie repeated, trilling the word to emphasize its power. "I call upon She Who Tends to honor my right of return. I no longer have my First Ashes from my former home." She raised her hands to show him the sampler threads. "Fortunately I had these to guide Smoky back home. Once again I have served the household. Isn't that enough to earn me a place here? I call upon She Who Tends, I call upon She Who Tends to swear I am right!"

A bright light flared. Then She Who Tends appeared, glaring at both of them.

"Who summons me?" she growled. He Who Had Stolen Her Place flinched back from She Who Tends's glower, but Dorakie faced She Who Tends without a tremor.

"I summoned you. Let me argue my case."

"Go ahead." She Who Tends's expression softened as she studied Dorakie. "I remember you. Dorakie, I named you. The little wood sprite too small to survive in the woods. I see you have thrived as a household sprite." Bewilderment crossed her face. "But this isn't your home."

"My First Ashes were destroyed." As She Who Tends frowned, Dorakie quickly explained what had happened. "So you see," she concluded. "I brought Smoky back to my old people. I seek refuge in this place."

"But I gave you a perfectly good tree!" He Who Had Stolen Her Place objected.

"A tree with unhealed rot!" Dorakie snapped back. "I mended it, no thanks to you!"

"Let me speak to the tree," She Who Tends said, cutting off He Who Had Stolen Her Place. "Nothing is to happen while I am gone. I *thought* I had things in order. Can't afford to be losing any more sprites, woods *or* household." She winked out of sight.

He Who Had Stolen Her Place sat, visibly tired. Dorakie looked around. She sensed a leaky pipe under the sink, and wandered over there.

"What are you doing?" he demanded.

"Pipes," Dorakie said. "They leak." She crawled through the gap between the cupboard doors under the sink to investigate. This was newer pipe than the previous house, but the joint was not completely sealed. She whispered a binding spell, forgetting that she did not have the right to mend things here.

Nonetheless, the dripping stopped. Dorakie traced through the rest of the plumbing. It was better than her old house, but oh, it still needed a sprite's touch to work right. She hummed softly to herself as she followed the water lines, learning the flow of the plumbing system here—

Then something grabbed her by her scruff, whisking her away from the plumbing and back into the kitchen. "What *are* you doing?" She Who Tends demanded, while He Who Had Stolen Her Place looked abashed.

"Oh, I—I—the pipes were dripping under the sink, so I fixed them," Dorakie said. "And I found other problems further on in the plumbing, so I..." Her voice trailed away as she saw the look on She Who Tends's face, as well as He Who Had Stolen Her Place.

"The plumbing listened to you?" She Who Tends asked.

"Yes." Smoky trotted past them with an intent look that Dorakie knew all too well. "Oh no you don't," she muttered, and whispered the *boundaries* spell to wrap around the outside cage. Smoky pushed through the flap and Dorakie followed her, watching as the cat headed for the hole, only to wander away from it looking confused.

"*Boundaries* worked for you here," She Who Tends said from behind Dorakie. "There is enough of your First Ashes in the things of your people that your spells work." She frowned thoughtfully. "You have a gift for house tending. Not all sprites do. I have lost so many." Sadness tinged her voice.

"But what about me?" He Who Had Stolen Her Place whined. "I age. I want to come inside."

She Who Tends looked thoughtfully around the yard. "Is this your work?"

He brightened. "Oh yes. I have cultivated this garden for years." He sighed. "But I find it hard to weave myself a warm, dry spot. When I felt First Ashes lingering in the things of these people, I hoped that I could use those Ashes to make myself welcome."

She Who Tends shook her head. "You do not have the gift for house tending. I am so sorry. I wish I could give it to you, along with a name."

His shoulders slumped. "I see," he said in a small voice. "But the people did love my garden. I will go back to it, though I do not know how much longer I can keep working."

"Wait," Dorakie said. She looked around the garden, remembering how Harriet especially had wanted a garden like this. "I could care for the house, and provide you with shelter while you tend the garden. We could help each other tend house and garden. Would you share this place with me?"

"I suppose." He looked hopefully at She Who Tends. "Would that be acceptable?"

"More than acceptable," She Who Tends said. "Dorakie, you are a generous and honorable sprite." She reached into her pocket and sprinkled dust onto Dorakie. "This will serve you as First Ashes from now on. Go and live where you will, and follow your heart into house tending."

"I will," Dorakie said.

She Who Tends turned to He Who Had Stolen Her Place. "As for you, nameless outdoor one. You will work with Dorakie to keep this house whole, inside and out." She sprinkled ashes over him. "I name you Flish. This serves you as First Ashes. Be named, and share space with Dorakie. Live in peace with one another."

"I will, She Who Tends. I swear by my first hollow and weave," Flish said.

"I'll help you find a warm space," Dorakie said. "Harriet will love having your help with the garden. I did some work but I—I'm better with the house."

"The tree spoke well of what you did for her, Dorakie,"

She Who Tends gently chided Dorakie. "Flish could use your aid in weaving protection."

"And Flish has an eye for organizing, based on what I saw in the garden," Dorakie said.

She Who Tends beamed. "I knew we could make this work!" She bent and kissed first Dorakie, then Flish, on their foreheads. "Live now in peace with one another." She vanished.

Dorakie and Flish looked at each other.

"I'm not sure how to start," Flish said. "I've always protected my space alone, not shared with another sprite."

"It's not the usual thing." Dorakie bit her lip, thinking. "But together, maybe we can keep each other safe from the *dogs*."

"And hawks," Flish said, frowning. "I've seen too many of our kind stolen by sharp-shinned hawks."

"We need safe dens," Dorakie said. "Nice, secure places." She shivered. "I never want to have a kobold like Walther invade my space again."

"Kobolds are dangerous," Flish agreed. He looked around. "I want a high den. Something where I can watch for invaders."

"Maybe the attic?" Dorakie suggested. She closed her eyes, taking stock of her new home. "Lots of insulation up there. You could make a nice cozy space by one of the soffit vents and—oh! Ick! Deal with the carpenter ants starting to move in! They're too far along for the *boundaries* spell."

"Ants?" Flish's voice brightened. "Let me at them! Upstairs, you said?"

"All the way up," Dorakie said, eyes still tightly shut as she visualized the location. "Under the gable, by that pine tree that's brushing the house."

"Oh, *that* one. Douglas fir that some stupid human

topped. I knew it had problems. I'll need your help to weave a protection for the tree."

"I will." Dorakie opened her eyes. "Fastest way up there is to go through the heating vents in the ceiling."

"I'm going to get myself some ants!" Flish crawled up the wall and into the heating vent, cackling to himself. "Tasty ants, tasty ants. Getting myself some tasty ants! Then make a bed, make a bed, make a bed. Tasty ants, make a bed. Make a bed, tasty ants."

Dorakie smiled as he disappeared, though she could hear him singing as he climbed into the attic. She looked around the kitchen. This house had a natural gas furnace and no fireplace. So where was she going to find herself a den?

The stove hood and fan caught her attention. She clambered into the fan's vent, slithering through the walls even though it tired her. A walled-off hollow space at the top of the cupboard was safely away from the fan's ductwork, but private enough for Dorakie. She would have to make a gap to get into her new den without slithering through walls—but otherwise, it was a lovely, warm space.

She heaved a big sigh and lay down on the boards. Soon enough her new den would be comfortable. But she was *home.*

Flish banged down the vent pipe. "Something for you," he called. "Do you have a door?"

"Not yet."

"Maggots! Oh well, those tasty ants did give me enough energy. May I enter?"

"Enter."

Flish pushed his way through the wall, tugging something through behind him. "I found these things. I know you house sprites like such trinkets! Here!" He pushed his double handfuls of fabric at Dorakie.

She sorted through them. One of Liz's hair ties. A holey sock from Harriet. And a small long-sleeved linen shift that didn't smell of either Harriet or Liz. It was just the right size for Dorakie to wear. She took a deeper whiff of it. Doll clothing? Possible.

"Thank you," she said finally, holding the shift up. "Where did you find this?

"In an attic corner, buried under insulation. I thought you might like it. It looked like something soft to sleep on."

"Or wear on a cold winter's night. Thank you," Dorakie repeated. "You found a home?"

"After eating tasty ants, yes! Just the right spot by a vent, lots of insulation to burrow into." He looked slightly abashed. "I took two socks from our people and kept the other one for my bed. I hope you didn't want both."

"No, no," Dorakie said. "You must make yourself comfortable as well." A strange warm feeling flowed through her as she spoke.

Love was not a common emotion among sprites, not with the need to protect their individual territories and the shorter lives that reproduction gave sprites. Dorakie was too old now and too weak to consider it. But humans cared for each other without procreating—like Harriet and Liz— and perhaps she and Flish could develop similar feelings as well.

"Thank you," Flish muttered. He ducked his head. "I'll be up in my den, if you want to come visit."

"I will, soon," Dorakie promised. After he left, she plumped up the sock to make herself a nice bed. Then she slid out of her den. Now to find an equally good present for Flish's space.

She looked forward to the opportunity to search out just the right thing for him.

ANOTHER EUROPEAN-BASED MYTHOLOGICAL CREATURE STORY. All of my friends were writing about fae, fairies, brownies, and what-have-you, so I gave it a try.

PREVIOUS PUBLICATIONS

"J.C. the Ski Bum" was previously published in *Fantasy Scroll Magazine* in 2014, and republished in *Dragons, Droids and Doom: Year One*, edited by Julian Ionescu and Frederick Root, Fantasy Scroll Press, 2015.

"The Wisdom of Robins" was previously published in *Whimsical Beasts*, edited by Sanan Kolva and Joyce Reynolds-Ward, Knotted Road Press, 2019.

"Breakthrough" was previously published in *Nightbird Singing in the Dead of Night,* edited by Jeff Dennis, Nightbird Publishing, 2009.

"River-Kissed" was previously published in *River*, edited by Alma Alexander, Dark Quest Books, 2011.

"Amulet, Cudgel" was previously published as "Gloriana" in *Artifact*, edited by Pam Bainbridge-Cowan, Lisa Cromwell, and Jadzia DeForest, Northwest Independent Writers Association, 2016.

"Meeting with Dragons" was previously published under the pseudonym "Lena Myrtle" in *Steam. And Dragons,* edited by Leah Cutter, Knotted Road Press, 2017.

"Coming Home" was previously published online in *Noctober*, 2009.

"Witch Trails" was previously published in *Allegory*, 2016.

"Queen of the Snows" was previously published in *Once Upon a Winter*, edited by H. L. Macfarlane, Macfarlane Lantern Publishing, 2021.

"Lost Loves" was previously published in *All Worlds Wayfarer*, 2019.

"Slow Dancing in 3/4 Zombie Time" was previously published in *Zombiefied,* edited by Carol Hightshoe, Sky Warrior Book Publishing, 2011

"The Notice" was previously published in *Children of a Different Sky,* edited by Alma Alexander, Kos Books, 2017.

"Safe Haven" was previously published in *Aurora Wolf,* 2019.

NEWSLETTER

Like what you've read? Want to follow Joyce either through her monthly newsletter or through an email feed of her irregular blog posts?

Sign up for Joyce's newsletter here:

https://tinyletter.com/JoyceReynolds-Ward

Or follow Joyce's irregular blog posts on her Substack, here:

https://joycereynoldsward.substack.com/

BOOKS AND PUBLICATIONS

The Martiniere Legacy

First Meetings: A Martiniere Legacy Short Story
Inheritance: The Martiniere Legacy Book One
Ascendant: The Martiniere Legacy Book Two
Realization: The Martiniere Legacy Book Three
A Belated Christmas Honeymoon: A Martiniere Legacy Short Story
The Enduring Legacy: The Martiniere Legacy Book Four

People of the Martiniere Legacy

The Heritage of Michael Martiniere: A Martiniere Legacy Novel
Broken Angel: The Lost Years of Gabriel Martiniere: A Martiniere Legacy Novel
Justine Fixes Everything: Reflections on Mortality

The Martiniere Multiverse

A Different Life: What If?
A Different Life: Now. Always. Forever.

Goddess's Honor titles currently available (chronological order):

The Goddess's Choice: A Goddess's Honor Short Story

Beyond Honor: A Goddess's Honor Novella

Exile's Honor: A Goddess's Honor Novelette

Birth of Sorrow: A Goddess's Honor Short Story

Pledges of Honor: Goddess's Honor Book One

Return to Wickmasa: A Goddess's Honor Short Story

Crown Anniversary: A Goddess's Honor Short Story

Challenges of Honor: Goddess's Honor Book Two

Cleaning House: A Goddess's Honor Outtake Story

Unexpected Alliances: A Goddess's Honor Rough Draft Outtake Story

Choices of Honor: Goddess's Honor Book Three

Judgment of Honor: Goddess's Honor Book Four

Netwalk Sequence Author Preferred 2022 Editions

Life in the Shadows: Book One

Netwalk: Book Two

Netwalker Uprising: Book Three

Netwalk's Children: Book Four

Learning in Space: Book Five

Netwalking Space: Book Six

Bright Star Fair Witches

Becoming Solo: A Bright Star Fair Witches Novella

Non-Series Titles currently available:

Alien Savvy: A Western SF Novella

Klone's Stronghold

Beating the Apocalypse

Bearing Witness

Fabulist and Fantastical Worlds: A Short Story Collection

Vella Titles:

Falcon of the Martinieres (part of *Justine Fixes Everything*)

Bearing Witness

Beating the Apocalypse

A Different Life—What If? An Alternative Martiniere Legacy Novel

Becoming Solo

A Different Life—Linda's Story: An Alternative Martiniere Legacy Novel

Federation Cowboy

Audiobooks Available:

Alien Savvy: A Western SF Novella

Released from other publishers:

"Queen of the Snows," in *Once Upon A Winter: A Folk and Fairy Tale Anthology*, edited by H. L. Macfarlane

"My Man Left Me, My Dog Hates Me, and There Goes My Truck," in *Black-Eyed Peas on New Year's Day: An Anthology of Hope*, edited by Shannon Page

"Lost Loves," in *All Worlds Wayfarer*

"The Wisdom of Robins," in *Whimsical Beasts: A Campcon Anthology*, edited by Joyce Reynolds-Ward

"The Cow at the End of the World," in *Well...It's Your Cow*, edited by Frog Jones

"To Plant or Pull Up Stakes," in *Pulling Up Stakes: A Campcon Anthology*, edited by Joyce Reynolds-Ward

"The Notice," in *Children of a Different Sky*, edited by Alma Alexander

About the Author

Joyce Reynolds-Ward has been called "the best writer I've never heard of" by one reviewer. Her work includes themes of high-stakes family and political conflict, digital sentience, personal agency and control, realistic strong women, and (whenever possible) horses. She is the author of *The Netwalk Sequence* series, the *Goddess's Honor* series, and the recently released *The Martiniere Legacy* series as well as standalones *Klone's Stronghold, Alien Savvy,* and *Beating the Apocalypse.* Samples of her Martiniere short stories/novel in progress and her nonfiction can be found on Substack at either Speculations from the Wide Open Spaces (general, writing) or Martiniere Stories (fiction). Joyce is a Self-Published Fantasy BlogOff Semifinalist, a Writers of the Future SemiFinalist, and an Anthology Builder Finalist. She is the Secretary of the Northwest Independent Writers Association, a member of the Science Fiction and Fantasy Writers Association, and a member of Soroptimists International.

facebook.com/authorjoycerw

twitter.com/JoyceReynoldsW1

instagram.com/jreynoldsward